Bestselling author Tori Carrington introduces
Private Scandals, a new miniseries filled with lust,
betrayal...and scandal like you've never seen it!

When Troy, Ari and Bryna Metaxas realize their
business—and family—is on the brink of ruin,
how far will they go to save them?

Find out in...

Private Sessions
(October 2010)

Private Affairs
(November 2010)

Private Parts
(December 2010)

Blaze™

Dear Reader,

Our Private Scandals miniseries was inspired by Homer's epic poem, *The Iliad;* the three stories a modern retelling of age-old conflicts, where love is the ultimate prize...and battles are fought in the bedroom, as well as the boardroom. And nowhere is that truer than in this final book....

In *Private Parts*, the last thing hot businessman Troy Metaxas wants is a sexy woman custom-made to drive him mad with desire. He's been so focused on his goal of bringing his hometown of Earnest, Washington, back from the brink of economic ruin that his personal life has gone long neglected. Kendall is Troy's match in every way, fueling his appetite for her lush body with every kiss. The problem is, the more time he spends in bed with her, the less focused he is on business. Especially when he discovers that she is the Trojan horse sent to bring him down....

We hope you enjoy Troy and Kendall's bone-melting journey toward sexily-ever-after. We'd love to hear what you think. Contact us at P.O. Box 12271, Toledo, OH 43612 (we'll respond with a signed bookplate, newsletter and bookmark), or visit us on the web at www.toricarrington.net.

Here's wishing you love, romance and HOT reading.

Lori & Tony Karayianni

aka Tori Carrington

Tori Carrington

PRIVATE PARTS

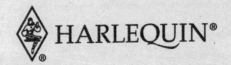

HARLEQUIN®

TORONTO • NEW YORK • LONDON
AMSTERDAM • PARIS • SYDNEY • HAMBURG
STOCKHOLM • ATHENS • TOKYO • MILAN • MADRID
PRAGUE • WARSAW • BUDAPEST • AUCKLAND

Recycling programs
for this product may
not exist in your area.

ISBN-13: 978-0-373-79584-0

PRIVATE PARTS

ABOUT THE AUTHOR

Multi-award-winning, bestselling authors Lori Schlachter Karayianni and Tony Karayianni are the power behind the pen name Tori Carrington. Their more than forty-five titles include numerous Harlequin Blaze miniseries, as well as the ongoing Sofie Metropolis comedic mystery series with another publisher. Visit www.toricarrington.net and www.sofiemetro.com for more information on the duo and their titles.

Books by Tori Carrington

We dedicate this book to every man who believes himself immune to love—and every woman who's endeavored to prove him wrong....

And to our magnificent editor, Brenda Chin, who feels it necessary every now and again to warn us to be careful about boundaries, even as she wholeheartedly cheers us on while we push against them!

_1_

"WHAT MAKES YOU THINK he's not just asking us to bend over so he can stick it in and break it off?"

Troy Metaxas stared at his younger brother across the diner table, his cup halfway to his mouth. Trust Ari to phrase the question that way.

He put his coffee down and sat back in the red leather booth. The Quality Diner was decked out for the coming holidays, with the struggling owner partial to the more whimsical themes of snowflakes and icicles, probably because they saw so little of either here in the Pacific Northwest. A white, papier-mâché angel hung above their booth, lazily spinning first one way and then the other.

He'd be lying if he said the possibility that Manolis Philippidis was planning to do just as Ari was suggesting hadn't crossed his mind. It had. At least a thousand times a day. But ever since the wealthy Greek businessman had reestablished contact with him a week ago, offering an olive branch on top of the contract that Troy had been trying to close...well, he'd been forced to listen.

He knew what he was getting into. But this project was important to him. After the family lumber mill closed over four years ago, he'd felt responsible for providing the town of Earnest with another employer. Then luck had met persistence and he'd come across an idea worth pursuing in emerging green technology. The solar panels the new company would produce would not only revolutionize the industry by capturing a wider array of the sun's rays, the thin-film method was also cost-saving, meaning more could afford the product.

A win-win situation all the way around.

He considered his brother. "So long as we finally get the project off the ground, what does it matter?"

"So your advice is to smile and take it?"

"That would be exactly my advice." He leaned forward. "Take a look around you, Ari. The unemployment rate in Earnest has risen to nearly thirty-five percent. And that doesn't count the residents forced to leave because they've lost their homes or had to relocate to find work."

He watched his brother look around the interior of the diner. It was a Wednesday morning and there were only a few people inside where once it would have been full of lumber mill workers catching breakfast before heading to work. Hell, five years ago, the midnight shift would just be knocking off and doing the same before going home.

"Half the businesses outside this diner have closed, with another quarter in danger of doing the same," he said. "Don't you think the town's worth a little discomfort?"

He didn't mention the exact reason for the collapse in negotiations between Philippidis and the Metaxas brothers six months ago. He didn't have to. Because the reason sat across from him. Ari's seduction and then stealing of Philippidis's bride on the evening before their wedding was the reason why the vital business arrangement had gone awry.

Even though it all seemed like yesterday to him, he had to keep in mind that Ari was now engaged to Elena Anastasios, and that she was entering into her third trimester with their child. No longer Philippidis's stolen bride, but Troy's soon-to-be sister-in-law and mother to his niece or nephew.

Ari shook his head now, as if in answer to his unsaid thoughts. "Considering all that no good SOB has done to us over this past half year, I would think the last thing we would want is to get into bed with him."

Troy didn't blink.

Ari raised his hands as if in surrender. "Okay, bad analogy. But you know what I mean. Who's to say this isn't just another set-up? That he's not going to string us along, get us to invest the few cents we have left, and then pull the rug out from under us again?"

"Who's to say he is?"

Ari remained dubious.

"Look, we've exhausted every other possibility. It's either this or we give up on the project altogether. That's not an option for me." Troy sipped from his coffee, the unsweetened liquid bitter against his tongue. "Anyway, we know who we're dealing with this time. And we're prepared for anything he can possibly throw our way."

Ari looked at his watch. Troy was as anxious as he was for the other three men scheduled to join them for breakfast to arrive. Because it meant that they were that much closer to the meeting they were to have with Philippidis at the mill offices later that morning.

The old cowbell above the door clanged. Troy glanced over his shoulder. It wasn't any of their three breakfast mates. It was a woman in black, close-fitting running pants and an oversize University of Oregon sweatshirt, looking more fit than he felt, her blond hair twisted into a knot at the back of her neck. She stripped the sweatshirt off, revealing the clingy tank she wore underneath.

Troy's gaze drifted over her nicely outlined curves. From her calves, up past her firm thighs, her rounded hips and then to where her breasts were two perfect half-globes under the damp fabric.

"Good morning!" Verna called out from the kitchen window. "Take a seat anywhere."

The latest addition was slightly out of breath as she voiced her thanks and chose the booth behind Troy, causing his seat to jostle a bit. He nearly spilled the coffee he was holding.

"Sorry," she said.

"No problem."

Troy looked to find Ari grinning at him.

"What?"

His brother shook his head. "Did I say anything? Because I don't think I did."

Troy grimaced. Since when had it become a crime to appreciate a woman's form? Especially seeing as it had been so long since he'd allowed himself the luxury. That and there hadn't been much opportunity. When you lived in the same small town you'd grown up in, and knew just about everyone, it was hard to stare at a woman's breasts and think of anything having to do with sex. It seemed a bit too…incestuous somehow, considering you knew her husband and kids and her parents and grandparents, not to mention that she used to wear braces or had a habit of drinking one beer too many on Friday nights at the pub.

Although he did have to admit he'd found himself doing exactly that lately, ogling the locals. How long had it been since he'd been on a proper date? Screw proper, when was the last time he'd lost himself in the scent of a woman's neck? Buried himself in her sweet flesh? Far longer than he cared to admit. And his body was apparently no longer willing to allow him to ignore it.

Just as soon as he got this contract nailed down, he'd dust off his little black book and call up a willing female or two in Seattle and go out on a date, he promised himself.

"Oh, you are in a sorry state, aren't you?" Ari asked. "How long has it been, anyway?" His dark brows rose high on his forehead. "Please don't tell me since Gail."

Troy squinted at him and leaned forward, indicating that he should lower his voice. With so few customers in the place, there was little doubt the woman behind him had heard what his brother had said.

"Later," he muttered.

"Well, that's the problem, isn't it, bro? It's always later with you." Ari leaned forward as well, but he didn't lower his voice. "Face it, you need to get laid."

The woman coughed. Troy looked to find her in the middle of sipping a glass of water, the contents of which she nearly spewed across the table in front of her.

"Cute," he muttered. "Very cute."

"Just sayin'," Ari said with a shrug.

Diner owner Verna Burns, who was also serving as the waitress, approached the woman's table and offered her coffee from the pot she held. Judging by the sounds, the woman accepted.

"Oh, Ari?" Verna said. "Thank Elena for that platter of baklava for me, will you? It was gone within a blink. Everyone loves it."

Before his brother could tell her he would pass on her sentiments to his fiancée, the telephone began ringing in the back of the diner. Verna hurried off to answer it with an apology.

"Elena's making baklava for the diner?" Troy asked.

Ari's grin disappeared. "She's still interested in buying the place."

"And apparently you're still against it."

"We're going to have a baby in three months. How is she going to handle that and this place?"

"Women have been balancing both since the beginning of time, Ari."

"Yeah, well."

Troy felt a tap on his shoulder. He turned to look into their neighbor's amused face. Her green eyes were bright, her cheeks brushed with color, her mouth full and smiling. "I'm sorry. Can I bother you for a little sugar?" she asked.

Oh, he'd like to give her a little sugar, all right.

"Sure." Troy picked up the container and handed it

to her, noting that her nails were neat and manicured, white half moons on the tips.

"Thanks."

He refused to look at Ari as he turned back, but couldn't ignore his quiet chuckle.

"Not a word," he muttered.

"Pardon me?" the woman asked.

"What? Oh. I'm sorry. I was talking to my brother."

"I see. I'm sorry to bother you again, but is that fresh cream there on your table? If it is, it's much better than this powdered stuff."

It took Troy a moment to process her request. When he reached for the cream, Ari was holding it out for him. He took it and nearly spilled the contents on the woman because he wasn't paying attention.

"Sorry," he said.

"No harm, no foul," she said with that same knowing smile.

"Good going, hot shot," his brother said.

Troy glared at him.

The woman again. "I suppose since we're having coffee together, I might as well introduce myself." She held out a slender hand. "Kendall Banks."

He shook her hand. "Troy Metaxas. This is my brother Ari. Although I'm considering disowning him."

She laughed as she shook Ari's hand, as well.

"Ah, the famous Metaxas brothers. Nice to meet you both."

"Are you from here?" Ari asked, much to Troy's chagrin.

"No, no. Just visiting your fine town."

"Staying at Foss's Bed and Breakfast?"

"Yes. How did you know? Oh. Never mind. It's probably the only place in town, isn't it?"

"Yes, it is."

"Where are you from?" Ari asked.

"Portland."

Troy wanted to reach across and stuff a paper napkin in his brother's mouth, anything to keep him from continuing the conversation.

"I'll let you two get back to your breakfast. Oh, wait." She held out the cream and sugar. "You can have these back. Thank you."

"Sure," Troy said, putting them back on the table.

Something outside the window thankfully caught Ari's attention. "Is that Palmer?"

Troy followed his gaze to see Palmer DeVoe, one of the three due to meet them for breakfast, along with Caleb Payne and Graham Johnson, the company's longtime attorney, coming out of Penelope Weaver's shop. He was grinning and shaking his head as he stopped on the sidewalk. Then he glanced in the direction of the diner and began crossing the street.

Palmer came inside and Troy stood to greet him, shaking hands with the man he'd once played varsity football with, but more recently had been his business adversary. Until Palmer had closed down his operation and offered to come on board with them.

Troy was convinced that the latest of Philippidis's key players to jump ship was to credit for the Greek's about-face. Well, that and the fact that Caleb Payne's mother, whom Philippidis had recently been dating, had reportedly dumped him when her son objected to the union.

Whatever the reason, Troy was glad for the chance to reunify with the Greek. The way he saw it, it was better to have him as a wary friend than an angry enemy. Philippidis had thrown up so many roadblocks in their efforts to secure funding to convert the lumber mill into a manufacturing plant that would produce solar panels, he'd almost abandoned all hope.

Then Philippidis had contacted him and asked for a meeting to see if they couldn't finally work things out.

The offer couldn't have come at a better time.

Palmer nodded toward the woman behind Troy as he sat down in the booth next to him.

Ari grinned. Troy grimaced.

"Where are Caleb and Graham?" Palmer asked, taking the hint.

"They should be here any minute." There was a

glint of sunlight off metal. "Speak of the devils. I think they just pulled up."

"Good," Troy said.

The sooner they were on with this, the better...

2

THREE HOURS LATER, TROY stood in his office, the telephone plastered to his ear. He was trying to convince a supplier to wait one week longer for the go-ahead on an order he'd placed half a year ago.

Barely visible to him were his surroundings.

He'd grown up in the old lumber mill. Had hid under the metal desk to his right that once belonged to his father and his grandfather before him. Had pressed his nose against the glass walls on three sides of the office, and written his name in the fog circle of condensation from his breath on the multi-paned windows through which thick forests could be seen. Had played on the iron-wrought catwalk and stairs that overlooked the open mill space below—a large area that used to buzz with activity but was now quiet, the old equipment kept more for sentimental reasons than any real use.

Every now and again Troy would catch the scent

of wood chips, reminding him of times gone by. But mostly he was too focused on the future to notice it or much about his surroundings.

"I'm going to have to go up on the price," the sales rep said.

Troy rubbed his closed eyelids. When he opened them back up, his gaze fell on the Christmas card he'd received in today's mail. From his ex-girlfriend, Gail. And his ex-best friend, Ray. Who were now a married couple sending out holiday cards together.

"Look," he said into the phone. "My secretary is motioning me into a meeting. Let me get back to you later today or early tomorrow..."

He quickly wrapped up the call and stood for a long moment trying to regain his bearings while he stared at the Christmas card. Lately, his days were full of like phone conversations. And they were beginning to take a toll on him. He'd talked his way around, out of and into so many corners he'd considered investing in a sledgehammer.

"You ready?" Ari asked from the open doorway, standing alongside Patience, his secretary.

Troy glanced through the glass. The conference room was at the far end of the wide elevated walkway, five glass-walled offices in between, while another five lay on the other side of his own office. Meeting participants were milling around, getting coffee and talking to each other. He hadn't even noticed them come in. Which was saying something, because they would have had to walk by his office.

His gaze went to Manolis Philippidis, who was the only one sitting. He was drumming his fingers against the table and looking at his watch.

Troy tossed the unopened greeting card into the wastebasket, accepted a file from Patience and followed his brother to the meeting room.

After greeting everyone else, he finally stood in front of Philippidis. He extended his hand, half expecting the Greek to ignore him. Instead, he was surprised when he got to his feet and returned the handshake.

"Let's do business," Troy said, feeling twenty pounds lighter as he took his seat at the head of the table.

"Sorry I'm late," a female voice said from the doorway.

Troy looked up to see a beautiful, leggy blonde enter the conference room. A familiar beautiful, leggy blonde.

He nearly fell into his chair as the woman who had introduced herself as Kendall Banks earlier at the diner shook hands with Philippidis and then the rest of the table before presenting herself to him.

Outside of her name, it was the sexy smile that linked her to the woman he'd met earlier. Otherwise, she looked completely different. Her hair was loose around her shoulders, a warm, golden blonde.

She wore makeup that accentuated her green eyes and complemented her naughty mouth, but didn't overwhelm her pretty face. And she'd exchanged her running pants and tank for a plum-colored suit with a short skirt, her long legs made longer still by the black heels she wore.

Troy found himself tugging at his collar as he took her hand.

"Hello again," she said with the hint of a smile.

Suddenly, his collar wasn't the only item of clothing that had grown tight.

"Sorry I'm late," she said to the room at large, tugging her gaze from his and walking around the table to the only free seat. "I was pulled over by your local sheriff for speeding and…well, afterward I really needed to speed, but didn't dare."

Chuckles and laughs.

"Did Barnaby ticket you?" Ari asked.

Kendall's smile was wide and unapologetic. "Of course not."

Philippidis cleared his throat. "Miss Banks will be the point man…or woman, rather, in putting this deal together. Seeing as my regular point men—" he looked over at Palmer and Caleb "—are now working for you."

Troy couldn't seem to take his gaze away from Kendall's face where she'd taken the seat at the far end of the table. The brief arch of her right brow told him she hadn't known about the little detail her boss had just shared. Did that mean she was also in the dark about the history behind their business dealings?

Ari was the one to clear his throat this time. "Troy?"

He blinked and stared at his brother.

"Oh, yes. Right." He opened his file and his secretary took her cue and began handing out the notes he'd had printed up. "If you'll refer to page two, paragraph four…"

THREE HOURS AND A CATERED working lunch later, Kendall lingered at the conference table rewriting notes that didn't need rewriting while the other meeting attendees left one by one.

Finally, she and Troy were alone in the room.

She slowly closed her leather-bound notebook and sat back in her chair, watching as he walked from the door where he'd just seen off his brother to the window overlooking the grounds to her right.

"Did this used to be a mill?" she asked, appreciating the fit of his navy blue suit, rather than their surroundings.

When they'd met earlier at the diner, she'd been instantly struck by how hot Troy Metaxas was. Intensely so. And his conversation with his brother before the others had arrived had amused her to no end.

So there was no one currently in Mr. Troy Metaxas's

life then? Good news for her. Because there was no one in her life, either. Not after her last boyfriend had taken a powder, saying something about her being too forward for him, too outspoken.

How was she supposed to know that his mother hadn't been aware that he'd lost his job three months ago?

Well, she did now. And Kendall was currently without a boyfriend. But seeing as they'd only dated for four months, she wasn't really crying in her chardonnay.

"Yes." Troy finally answered her question as he turned from the window. "My family owned this lumber mill for nearly a century before closing it for good four years ago."

She nodded. "I like that you're holding on to the history."

She'd moved her chair back from the table and slowly crossed her legs. Troy stood to her right, giving him a bird's-eye view of her suggestive movements.

He didn't disappoint as he leisurely took in the line of her legs. She worked hard on them, tried to run at least three miles, four times a week, so she knew they were fantastic. And wasn't averse to using them to their full advantage.

"So how long have you been working for Philippidis?" he asked.

She raised her brows. "How long? Well, that's a complicated question."

He waited.

"You see, I don't actually work directly for Manolis. He brought me on board especially for this project."

She didn't understand his grimace. "And you've known him for...how long?"

She rubbed the front of her shoe against the back of her opposite calf. "I've been familiar with him for, oh, about eight months or so. He helped my father out with our law firm in Portland."

"He owns it," he stated rather than asked.

"Yes. Manolis currently owns it. But my father's hoping to buy it back at some point."

"I'd tell him not to hold his breath."

"Oh, the hostility." She put her notebook into her briefcase. "I picked up on it during the meeting. What's the history here?"

Troy scrubbed his hair back from his forehead. The telltale sign made him all the more attractive to her. "It doesn't matter."

He looked at her again, but she couldn't tell if it was because he was interested, or if he'd rather she'd left.

"What are you doing here?" he asked.

"I'm not sure I understand."

He gestured toward the table. "I don't mean to cast a shadow on your qualifications, but—"

"But you're casting a shadow."

He didn't blink.

Kendall slowly uncrossed her legs and got to her feet. She collected her briefcase and sauntered over to him. "Rest assured, Mr. Metaxas, I'm very, very good at what I do."

"Troy. Please."

She stood within breathing distance of him and she noticed the way he seemed to inhale her scent.

Hot. Definitely hot.

"As to why I, um, stayed behind after the meeting…" She allowed her gaze to skim over his tall, solid form. "Well, I won't lie to you, Troy. Ever since we crossed paths this morning, before I knew who you were, I've been attracted to you."

He cleared his throat, apparently not as unaffected by her presence as he'd like her to think. "I don't mix business with pleasure, Miss Banks."

"Kendall, please." She smiled. "And I don't mix business with pleasure, either. My business *is* my pleasure." She slid her free hand inside the lapel of his suit jacket, running her fingertips along the expensive material, and the back of her knuckles against his tight abs through his broadcloth shirt.

He inhaled sharply.

"And I happen to think that we can be as successful in the bedroom as in the boardroom…"

3

THE WOMAN WAS DOWNRIGHT distracting. And for the life of him, Troy couldn't decipher whether that was a good thing or a bad thing.

Bad thing. Definitely a bad thing.

More than at any time in the past year, it was important for him to give his full attention to pulling this contract together. And thoughts of Kendall Banks's long, long legs weren't helping him do that.

To the contrary, they were inspiring him to think of a different business altogether. Monkey business.

"Would you like a cheese plate with dinner?"

"Huh?" Troy registered that he stood in the kitchen of the large Metaxas estate, and that Thekla Kalomiris, the housekeeper—who, along with her husband of thirty-five years, Frixos, took care of everything at the house and surrounding property—was talking to him.

He looked down at the cold beer bottle in his hand, barely remembering taking it out of the refrigerator.

"A cheese plate," the Cypriot turned American citizen repeated. "Would you like one to go along with dinner tonight?"

He squinted at her.

"Roast lamb."

"Ah. No. No, I don't think that's necessary, Miss Thekla. Thank you."

He wandered into the connected dining room, looking out the French doors at the expansive deck that offered one of the most stunning views in Washington State.

"Long day," Ari commented, coming to stand next to him.

"No longer than any other."

"Come on. Even you have to be stressed after that meeting earlier."

Ari turned toward the large table that could easily seat eighteen but was set for six tonight.

"Actually, I'm relieved."

"Bullshit."

This from another meeting attendee, Caleb Payne, who, in addition to being Philippidis's ex-employee, was also dating Troy and Ari's younger cousin Bryna, thus explaining his presence at a family dinner.

Caleb poured a finger of whiskey into a cut crystal glass and then took a long pull. "That despot is up to something. I know it."

Troy held his gaze. "Well, if anyone would be familiar with the way Philippidis operates, it's you, Caleb." He raised his beer to him. "That's why I like having you on this side of the table. If you spot anything unusual, speak up."

"Oh, trust me," Bryna said, taking the glass from Caleb's hand and downing the remainder of the contents. "He will. I swear, it's all he talks about lately. Nonstop. Even in bed."

"Oh, TMI," Ari said, raising his hand.

"I concur," Troy agreed.

Bryna smiled widely, apparently having gotten in her daily jab that made the brothers cringe at how quickly she was growing up. More than a cousin, she was like their younger sister considering she'd been raised by their father after her parents died when she was twelve.

"What does TMI mean?" the elder Metaxas asked as he entered.

The four looked at each other before bursting out laughing.

"Never mind, Dad," Ari said, pulling out the chair at the head of the table for him. "Just another acronym that will be passé before you have a chance to commit it to memory."

Percy Metaxas grimaced as he sat down. "Damn kids. Always reinventing the wheel."

"Not reinventing, exactly," Bryna said, taking the seat to his left. "Just adding a little oil every now and again." She briefly squeezed his hand. "I'm sure you got great use out of your own oil can when you were our age."

Percy's grin was large. "Nothing that I can repeat in polite company."

Troy considered his half-empty beer bottle and placed it on the bar. "Since when are any of us considered polite?"

Percy looked around the table. "Isn't there someone missing?" Finally his gaze settled on Ari. "Where's Elena?"

Troy tried to hide his frown as he took the seat to his father's right. Would there ever come a time when he'd hear her name and not instantly remember what had happened six months ago?

He could only hope that his renewed business dealings with Philippidis would provide him that relief. Because it wasn't doing him or his brother any good to continue to hold on to past grievances.

"She'll, um, be here in a minute," Ari said, taking a seat two up from Troy, leaving the one between them for his fiancée.

As if on cue, the woman in question hurried into the room. "Ari's too much of a gentleman to share that I can't seem to hold my liquor anymore." She ran her elegant fingers over her swollen belly. "Sometimes it seems her favorite place is resting against my bladder."

"His," Ari said. "And what do you mean liquor?"

"She didn't mean literally, cousin," Bryna said, shooting him an eye roll. "Elena probably hasn't tasted a drop of alcohol since she got pregnant. She loves that baby even more than she loves you, I think."

Ari looked panicked where he held out a chair for Elena.

She laughed. "Impossible. I might be able to love our child as much as…but I could never love her more," she said.

Ari appeared instantly relieved. "Him. You could never love him more."

"Why don't you two just find out the gender and be done with it?" Percy asked. "It was cute for the first five minutes, but it's starting to irritate even me now." His smile softened his words. "Besides, I'd like to know which sex my first grandchild is."

"Sorry, Dad. You're just going to have to wait like the rest of us," Ari said.

Troy sat back, silently watching them interact. The roast leg of lamb was offered up with potatoes, with Bryna helping Miss Thekla serve. The cook refused to join them when they invited her to sit, as she did every time the invitation was extended. They all knew she preferred to take her meals with her husband in their suite of rooms just off the kitchen.

Everyone conversed easily, with Bryna touching Caleb's sleeve every now and again, and Ari talking to the baby growing in Elena's belly. The elder Metaxas seemed to enjoy dinner in a way that he hadn't done since Troy's mother had passed away. The more people that were added to the table, the happier he seemed to grow. And that afforded Troy a measure of relief that no number of successful business deals ever could.

For a time, he and Ari had been concerned that they hadn't lost just one parent, but both, with Percy sinking into some sort of listless funk which none of them seemed capable of helping him out of. His interest in the family business waned, interaction with his two sons was rare outside his occasionally showing up at the dinner table, and Troy had worried that his only wish was to join his wife in the great hereafter.

Then, just before Troy and Ari had traveled to Greece, Percy was diagnosed with prostate cancer... and he'd decided not to be treated for it.

Troy understood that it was a viable option. That his cancer was slow growing and wasn't likely to be the cause of the end of his life. But it had created enough of a scare for his two sons and niece.

Then a pregnant Elena had accepted Ari's marriage proposal and was spending more and more time at the house. And Bryna had insisted that they accept Caleb even before he had crossed enemy lines.

And just like that, Percy Metaxas seemed to have found a new lease on life.

"You should have seen him," Ari was saying, making Troy realize that he'd zoned out from the conversation. "His tongue was practically dragging on the floor."

Troy narrowed his gaze, hoping his brother wasn't talking about him.

"And then," Bryna said, putting her hand on Caleb's shoulder to pre-empt him from saying something first. "He completely forgot where he was. Ari had to remind him that there was a meeting he needed to conduct."

Troy nearly choked on the lamb he was in the middle of swallowing.

Percy chuckled. "Troy? Our Troy? Impossible. No one is capable of throwing him off his game. Especially not a woman."

"Oh, but this isn't just any woman, Mr. Metaxas. This one—" Caleb's words stopped as Bryna elbowed him in the ribs. He chuckled good-naturedly and put his arm around her, pulling her back against his front. "This one is tailor made for Troy."

Ari chimed in, "Light to his dark, and just as tenacious."

Tenacious? Troy wasn't sure he'd use the word to describe Kendall Banks. He remembered the way she'd brushed the back of her knuckles against his taut stomach and grinned. Well, okay. It wasn't the only word he'd use to describe her.

He blinked to find everyone staring at him.

"What?" he fairly croaked.

A heartbeat later, the entire table erupted in laughter at his expense.

And he joined in.

KENDALL REASONED THAT she probably should have gone home. It was nine-thirty on a Friday night and all was not well.

She sat in her room at the bed and breakfast, listening to the complete silence around her. Mrs. Foss, the owner, had long since disappeared to her own rooms downstairs, and it seemed the entire town had retired for the evening.

She supposed it would be a pretty good bet that the single pub on Main Street would have some business. But she couldn't seem to generate any enthusiasm for a solo outing.

She squeezed lotion into her hand and rubbed it over her left leg, repeating the ritual with the other. She'd taken a shower and wore undies and a short pink robe her sister had gotten her last Christmas. She put the lotion bottle on the nightstand and sighed. She could always get dressed and drive home to Portland now. Spend the weekend doing the holiday shopping she still needed to see to. Lord knew nothing was going on here. Meetings were suspended until Monday.

And it was becoming increasingly clear that yummy Troy Metaxas intended to honor his belief that you shouldn't mix business with pleasure, no matter how overtly she flirted with him.

She flopped back onto the mattress, twirling the robe's silky belt around her finger.

Okay, so she wasn't used to such rejection. Not that she got every man she set her sights on, but having to face that man every day took its toll on a girl.

She should have gone home.

She pushed up off the bed, looked for her slippers, couldn't find them, then stepped to the door, quietly cracking it open. Caleb Payne was also staying in the bed-and-breakfast in the room at the end of the hall, but she hadn't seen him come back yet. And guessed he might not, seeing as he and Bryna Metaxas seemed to have something hot and heavy going on.

Otherwise, the place was quiet and empty.

Padding silently down the hall and then the stairs, she wondered where Mrs. Foss had stored the homemade apple pie she'd offered her a piece of earlier. Just a small slice, she told herself. Something decadent to make up for the other decadent somethings she might have had if Troy wasn't so damn stubborn.

She knew he wanted her. Saw it in his eyes every time their gazes met. So why was he fighting so hard? Why didn't he just give in and enjoy what she was offering up? A little no-strings sex never hurt anybody. In fact, it usually helped.

Kendall certainly could use some right about now.

A floorboard in the foyer creaked under her foot. She made a face and tried to be a little more careful, staying just to the side of the well-traveled paths of the old house in the hopes that she wouldn't run into another old board determined to give away her intentions.

The fanlight above the oven was on in the kitchen. And right there on top of the stove sat what she was looking for, covered in plastic wrap.

Oh, yes. A piece of apple pie would definitely hit the spot right now.

She quietly got out a dish and served herself up a helping, wondering if there was any ice cream to be had with it. Bingo! She took a carton of French vanilla from the freezer, scooped some out and then put it away.

Mmm…

Nothing was so good as a forbidden treat indulged in when nobody was looking.

She began padding her way back to her room, licking her fork, when a shadow appeared at the doorway.

Her heart skipped a beat as she recognized who it was. And it wasn't Caleb. Rather it was a treat better than homemade apple pie, even with ice cream.

Troy Metaxas...

4

HE SHOULDN'T HAVE COME.

Troy stood on the porch of Foss's B and B just outside the arc of light created by the fixture over the door and considered his options. If he knocked, Mrs. Foss would very likely be the one to answer. And he wasn't sure he wanted to face her this late on a Friday night.

The town as a whole had been surprised at best, mystified at worst when the Fosses had first decided to turn their six-bedroom house into a bed-and-breakfast about a decade ago. They had eight kids, all of who had moved out of town as soon as they came of age because their parents had been so overprotective they were barely allowed out of the yard until they were eighteen.

Then Mr. Foss had died and Mrs. Foss continued on, twice as miserable as before. While Troy ran into her only on the rare occasion, none of his encounters with her had been particularly pleasant. Partly because she blamed his family for the loss of her children to bigger cities after the shut-down of the lumber mill. Mostly because she was a bitch.

The thought of seeing her now seriously threatened whatever latent desires had brought him there in the first place.

He began to turn away when the door opened. He turned back, about to offer his apologies to the ornery old woman…and was instead presented with exactly the person who had haunted his dreams for the past three days.

Kendall.

"Hi," she said simply.

"Hi." He took her in from head to foot, thinking that she should wear that short, silky pink robe all the time. He'd have never been able to refuse her for as long as he had if he'd only seen this.

The deep V revealed that she wore no bra or camisole, her breasts soft, pale mounds. At least what he could see. What he couldn't see, he could easily guess at as her nipples poked against the fabric, drawing attention to the darker, puckered skin there. The hem of the robe hit her at just below what was decent, if decent could be used to describe any part of the sexy-as-all-get-out woman in front of him.

She shifted her weight from one bare foot to the other, causing her robe to open. He caught a glimpse of the lacy crotch of her white panties and nearly groaned aloud.

"Is there a particular reason you stopped by on this chilly night?" she asked with a saucy smile.

Oh, there was a really good reason. And it was looking straight at him...

KENDALL HAD TROY EXACTLY where she wanted him: in her bedroom.

Well, all right. Maybe not exactly where she wanted him. Because that would put him right between her thighs.

All good things come to those who wait...

She licked her lips, tasting vanilla ice cream there. "Would you like some pie?" she asked.

He still stood just inside the room in his overcoat, his gaze darting toward the closed door.

"Don't worry. Mrs. Foss sleeps like the dead."

His grimace was altogether too handsome. "Somehow I doubt that."

"You're right. She's probably listening to everything we say through a glass pressed to the wall." She'd put her plate down on a small table near the window that was flanked by two wicker chairs. She sat in one and adjusted her robe a beat slower than she should have. So shoot her. She was enjoying his reaction to her wanton actions a little too much. Her panties were already dripping and the silk rasped against her übersensitive nipples, eliciting a wicked shiver.

"Please. I'll share."

He looked back at the closed door again, then finally sat down. He seemed to realize he was still wearing his coat and got back up to take it off, carefully folding it over the back of the chair before sitting down again.

The sign of a true bachelor.

She took a slow, sinful bite of the pie, humming as she did so. "As sour as Mrs. Foss is, she makes a sweet apple pie."

"That's because she doesn't make it. Verna at the diner does."

Kendall raised her brows. "Thanks for the insider info." She smiled. "Does everyone know everyone else's business here in Earnest?"

"Pretty much."

She took another bite and pointed the fork in his direction. "So word will be all over about your visit then?"

"It will probably be on the front page of the *Earnest Gazette*. Along with a picture."

"Above or below the fold?"

"The *Gazette* doesn't have a fold. It's more of a newsletter."

She laughed as she held out a forkful of pie for him to take. He shook his head.

"No, thank you. I've eaten."

"What's that got to do with anything?"

"Good point." He took the fork and put the bite in his mouth.

Kendall crossed her legs again, well aware that when she moved, the skimpy bottom of her robe bowed open. At least until she closed the flaps again. She watched him have difficulty swallowing.

"So, that means you might as well do what you came here to do then…" she led.

He squinted at her in the dim light cast by the table lamp. "I'm not sure I'm following you."

Oh, he was going to follow her all right. Right into that bed.

"Well, if you leave now, the headline will read, 'Town Good Boy Stops in for a Quickie.'"

He began coughing. She handed him her glass of water.

She crossed her arms over her chest. "So we might as well get our front page's worth, don't you think?"

TROY HAD NEVER MET A woman as forward…or as hot…as Kendall Banks. Which was just as well, because he was having a hell of a time trying to carry on a casual conversation with her looking like sin incarnate, an all too inviting bed two steps away.

He stood up. She stood up. He raised his hand to the side of her face, marveling at the mercurial green of her eyes. One moment, lime, the next, almost brown. His gaze fastened on her full lips. He rubbed his thumb against the plump pillow that was her bottom one and then touched the pad to his own tongue, tasting vanilla ice cream.

"Now, this is more like—"

He kissed her mid-sentence, and their teeth knocked together. He winced and watched as she did the same. She leaned in, nearly kneeing him in the groin. He tilted his head the same way she did, then moved the other way at the same time. He tried kissing her again…and got her nose when she looked down at where he was slightly standing on one of her bare toes.

Finally, he lifted his hands up in surrender. If he'd needed any more proof that this wasn't a good idea, he'd just gotten it.

"Oh, don't even consider it, buster," she whispered.

She reached for his tie, loosened it and then took it off together. Then she worked on the first few buttons of his shirt before shoving him toward the bed. Luckily he landed on it, sitting on the edge, instead of on the floor.

Kendall slid her fingers under his chin, drawing his gaze to her eyes rather than to her breasts where they swayed against her robe, promising to come out to play.

"I think we can do better than that," she murmured. "In fact, I know we can…"

She bent down, pressing her mouth against his.

Sweet Jesus, but she tasted good. Like spiced apples and one hundred percent female.

"Relax," she whispered, pushing his shirt down over his arms without undoing the rest of the buttons, essentially trapping him in his own clothes. "You do know the meaning of the word, don't you, Mr. Metaxas?"

Oh, he knew the meaning, all right. He was just having a hard time applying it to the immediate circumstances. His erection pressed almost painfully against the front of his pants. A very hard time.

The way his brother and friends talked, he figured he was probably the only man on earth who had never had a one-night stand. The only women he'd been intimate with he had dated. Usually for a couple of months before he even got to second base, much less third.

The thought that he hadn't even taken Kendall out for coffee struck him as odd. As if what was happening were part of a dream instead of reality.

She pressed her fingers against his hard-on and he groaned.

This was so much better than any dream.

"Mmm. Told you," she murmured, kissing him again.

"Told me what?"

She forced his shoulders back until he was half

lying on the bed, his arms still pinned by his shirt. "Told you we could do this better."

She stood, her gaze plastered to his as she toyed with the belt fastened around her waist. Then she slowly untied it, allowing the silky material of the robe to fall away, exposing a narrow slip of her nudeness down to the thin scrap of white cotton that was her panties.

Kendall curved her fingers so that they rested inside the lapels and slid them up and down, her knuckles grazing her own skin.

Hot. So very, very hot.

"If I'd have known you were coming I would have worn sexier panties."

Troy forced a swallow down his impossibly tight throat. "I think what you have on is sexy enough."

Who was he kidding? He nearly came merely looking at the way the cotton clung to her springy curls.

She shifted her weight from one foot to the other, causing the fabric to move back and forth. "Do you think so?"

Troy nodded several times, not trusting his voice.

Kendall smiled and popped one of her shoulders out of the robe, then the other, as she held the material over her breasts.

He groaned. He was grossly unprepared for any

of this. He'd never even been to a strip joint, for God's sake.

Okay, maybe he had gone once. But it had been for a business meeting and he'd barely looked at the girls on stage. At least until one of them stuck her perfectly rounded bottom into his face. He'd been so embarrassed he hadn't known what to do, until his brother Ari handed him a five-dollar bill and indicated he should put it in her G-string.

He had. And the instant the stripper had moved away, Troy had called the meeting to an abrupt end.

Ari had teased him about that night for months afterward.

But Kendall…she was no strange stripper looking for a fiver to be tucked into her underpants. Although with her smoking body, she could easily qualify for the job.

She leaned over him, kissing him so thoroughly he forgot about G-strings and robes and just about everything else outside of his growing desire to be joined with her.

Now.

5

KENDALL HAD KNOWN HER share of guys. And while a couple of them had come close to Troy in the looks department, not a one could touch the passion that was written on every inch of him.

While she played at casual seduction, a deep, hot ball of wonderment began growing low in her belly. A sensation she wasn't familiar with but intrigued her no end.

There was just something about the way he looked at her. Allowed her to take control.

She broke their kiss and leaned back to tug his shirt from the waist of his slacks before hauling it up and over his head, releasing him from his temporary restraint. His gaze was solidly on her breasts as she worked and she couldn't help smiling at his fascination with such a basic part of the female anatomy. Her anatomy.

She tucked her fingers inside the waist of his

slacks. He drew in a deep breath. She might have believed he'd done it in order to make room for her. But in Troy's case, she suspected it was born of genuine surprise. Maybe not so much at her actions, but at his own reaction.

A sweep of her thumb opened the fastener and a tug brought the zipper down. He wore simple white briefs. No designer label that she could make out.

There was nothing simple, however, about the erection that sought freedom from the material.

She briefly lost her breath as she reached inside the front of his briefs, taking the length of him in her hand. Like the man himself, his penis was thick and hard and intense, the purple head looking somehow angry at having been caught off guard.

She stood back up and shrugged out of her robe, glad to be rid of it, having moved far beyond any seductive acts. She helped Troy out of the last of his clothing until he was a chiseled, breathing Greek god against the bed, every inch of him ripped and corded and bulging with life.

He grasped her hand and hauled her down on top of him. A destination she was all too willing to visit.

His skin was deliciously hot against hers, his hands probing and insistent. Gone was the awkwardness of earlier, replaced by curious exploration. She discovered that his inner thighs were particularly sensitive to her touch, while he learned that nuzzling the nape of her neck melted her bones.

He raised her hands above her head and then rolled her over, visually sweeping her body.

"God, you're beautiful."

She smiled. "Can we—um—save the commentary for later?"

His chuckle was low and sensual. "Not exactly modest, are you?"

She spread her legs wide. "Depends on what you consider modest…"

She watched as his expression darkened. She predicted he'd grab her hips and thrust deep inside her, which was exactly where she wanted him. Instead, he covered her womanhood with the span of his hand and gently squeezed.

Kendall nearly climaxed right then and there at the unexpectedness of the move.

She stretched her neck and restlessly ran her tongue along her lips as he stroked her.

So…so…nice…

When she felt his mouth against her clit, she nearly levitated from the bed.

Oh…yes…

In her cotton-stuffed brain, she couldn't recall the last time a guy had gone down on her. Everything was usually so rushed…so destination oriented. There never seemed to be time for more than brief foreplay.

But Troy...

He spread her swollen flesh wide and blew on her.

Troy seemed determined to prove himself better than the rest.

He took her stiff bud into his mouth again and applied suction.

And the gathering heat in Kendall's belly exploded...

FOR A WOMAN AS EXPERIENCED as Kendall appeared, she was amazingly responsive to his simple attempt to give her pleasure.

Troy wanted nothing more than to slide up her body and enter her then and there, to stake his claim on her, but he forced himself to stay where he was, leisurely lapping at her sensitive folds even as he inserted his index and middle fingers into her. Her slick muscles instantly gave way and then contracted around him, rippling evidence of her orgasm as he readied her for the next step in his own game of seduction.

To him, sex had never been about the end result; it was about savoring every last moment of the intimate connection. Whatever else might be said about him, it was widely accepted that he gave of himself one hundred percent in whatever he did.

And now his attention was focused solely on Kendall Banks.

When he suspected she was near climax again, he slowly withdrew his fingers, much to her consternation as she gave a small whimper and tried to close her thighs to keep him there. He smiled as he held her hips down with his hands and licked a trail up her trembling stomach, drawing damp circles around her breasts and suckling her pale nipples. She smelled of peaches and cream. Exactly how he might have imagined she would smell.

Finally, he was kissing her again. And found himself falling into the sensual heat of her mouth. He reached for the foil packet he'd taken out of his pocket before Kendall had stripped his pants from him and sheathed himself.

She immediately strained up against him, seeking relief. Instead, he ran the length of his erection down her dripping channel and back again, and then left it sandwiched between her swollen flesh, refusing her the joining she sought.

She made a small noise of disappointment and frustration and he kissed her deeply, smoothing her golden hair back from her face.

"Shh…" he said, appreciating the feel of her soft body under his even as she writhed in restless need.

He kissed her right eyebrow. Then her left. Drew his lips along the bridge of her nose, then bypassed her mouth for her chin. Slowly, ever so slowly, she began to relax. Still.

Better. Much better.

He nudged her thighs farther apart with his knee and then reached between them, caressing her before parting her flesh.

Then—finally—he entered her, sinking in to the hilt in one long, shudder-inducing stroke.

Her breath came out in a long rush. She curved her heels around his calves, taking him all in, her pupils large in her green, green eyes.

He kissed her full on the mouth. Only when he had her complete attention did he begin moving again.

A low moan emitted from her elegant throat, nearly taking whatever tenuous control he asserted over himself with it. He froze, listening to the *thud-thud* of his heartbeat, relishing every last sweet sensation of her, him and how it felt to be joined together.

Then he sank into her again.

"God…oh, God…" she whispered. "That feels so…good."

And it did. Having Kendall under him, around him, holding him was unlike anything he had imagined. And he'd done a lot of imagining over the past few days.

This…this magnificent reality…far surpassed anything he'd been able to conjure.

And that was saying a lot.

As he felt himself growing nearer his crisis, he

worked his hand between their bodies, smoothing his palm down over her belly, seeking, searching, until finally his fingers rested in her damp curls, finding his destination.

Kendall gasped and her body grabbed him tightly. Then, and only then, did he allow himself to let go...

MORE!

The word echoed through Kendall's mind as she fought to catch her breath.

"That...was...incredible..." she murmured, staring unseeingly at the wall opposite her. She shifted her gaze to stare into Troy's face as he lifted to his hands. So intense. So damn hot.

She smiled, the deep embers burning in her veins fanning back into flames. She gently hit his arms near the elbows, causing his arms to collapse and then rolled him over, the bed springs groaning as she straddled him.

Mmm...yes. That was more like it.

The expression of surprise and chagrin he wore was nearly her undoing as she leaned over to kiss him.

"What, you didn't think we were done, did you?"

He opened his mouth to respond but nothing came out. So she kissed him again. She discovered she was at risk of sliding over the side of the bed.

"Scoot up," she whispered.

He obeyed, the old mattress springs giving another squeak as they both moved nearer to the middle of the bed.

A sharp knocking on the floor below them caught them both off guard. They stared at each other, wide-eyed.

"Is that what I think it is?" Troy whispered.

Kendall nearly giggled. "I don't know. But there's one surefire way of finding out…"

She bounced up and down on top of him, giving the springs a good workout, then stopped, listening intently.

The banging came again.

She slapped a hand over her mouth to muffle her laugh while Troy used her shoulder.

She rolled over to lie next to him and they lay like that for long, long minutes, neither of them daring to move for fear it would incite another knock.

"I feel like I just got busted by my parents," Kendall said, brushing her hair back from her face.

"Tell me about it. Only, Mrs. Foss is every kid's nightmare. I wouldn't put it past her to come up here…"

His voice trailed off and then like that he was up and out of the bed.

Kendall raised herself to her elbows, watching him. "Where are you going?"

"Talk about your water buckets," he mumbled under his breath.

"We don't have to use the bed."

He looked around and then shifted his weight from foot to foot. The floorboards moaned. "Unfortunately, everything in this place makes too much noise."

Kendall stretched her leg out, running her big toe along his thigh as he buttoned his shirt. "Will I see you again?"

Troy's hands slowed as his gaze crashed with hers.

She shivered all over. Even without his saying anything, she saw it there in his handsome face. Oh, yes, she'd be seeing him again. Hopefully very soon...

6

"YOU'RE IN A GOOD MOOD."

Kendall's face was tilted up toward the tall ceiling of the Lloyd Center Mall back home in Portland, an hour-and-a-half drive from Earnest, marveling at the holiday decorations with all the wonder of one of her sister's two children.

Well, that would be true if four-year-old Mason wasn't yanking on his mother's leg, chanting the mantra, "I want the train, Mommy, I want the train," and if two-year-old Matilda weren't strapped into her stroller screaming at the top of her lungs that she didn't want to see Santa, looking like she was a growl away from turning her head three-hundred-and-sixty degrees.

Amazingly, Celia not only appeared unbothered by her children's demands, she looked…calm.

"I am happy," Kendall said with a wide smile.

And she was.

She'd woken up this morning in a tangle of bedding, Troy long gone but somehow still there, with her.

Last night...last night...

She found herself curiously without words. So she sighed instead.

"Okay, who is he, how long have you been seeing him and where does he work?" Celia asked.

While Kendall blinked at the question, her sister didn't miss a beat, wiping the tears from her daughter's red face and offering her a teething ring, before she handed Mason a toy train from a bag on the back of the stroller.

"Whatever do you mean?" Kendall asked, batting her eyes.

Celia laughed as they continued on, both children instantly, thankfully silent. "I figure it's either a guy or a juicy case. And since I already know that you're working a run-of-the-mill contract closing, it's got to be a guy."

"Since when have I been this happy about a guy?"

Celia's steps slowed as she took her in. "You're right. So who is he?"

Kendall laughed. She leaned over, unfastened her niece from her harness, and lifted the fussy toddler up into her arms.

"Oh, don't think a kid on your hip is going to

encourage me to change the subject," her sister warned.

Kendall pointedly talked to the two-year-old about overbearing older siblings and all the fun she had to look forward to being the younger child.

The Banks family wasn't large. Only their mother, father and the two girls. But what it lacked in size, it made up for in love. Kendall was hard pressed to remember a birthday, a holiday, a Sunday dinner they hadn't spent together. She was sure there had to be a few, but it was never because they didn't want to be together.

Laughter. There was and had always been a lot of it. Through life's highs and lows, scraped knees and broken hearts. Celia's marriage five years ago to her high school sweetheart and their father's business woes. They remained a cohesive unit, there for each other through every twist and turn.

And they always shared everything.

Which made Kendall's desire to keep Troy all to herself all the more curious.

"Give," Celia demanded.

"There's really nothing to give," she admitted.

Because she'd gotten what she wanted. Sex. That's what she'd proposed to Troy. And that's what she'd gotten. Pure and simple.

Only there was nothing simple about it. What he'd done last night...

She shivered merely thinking about.

"I'm waiting," her sister reminded her.

Kendall strapped little Matilda back into her stroller. "Are we shopping or are we playing twenty questions?"

"Both."

She laughed. "Yes, well, this is just going to have to be one of those times when you don't get what you want, Cel. Now, where did you say that green sweater was that you wanted to get for Dad?"

Her sister looked at her long and hard, and then a slow smile spread across her face.

"What?" Kendall asked.

Celia shook her head. "Nothing."

"Don't give me nothing. You're obviously thinking something. That evil expression is giving you away."

"There's nothing evil about my thoughts or my expression."

"That's up to interpretation."

"It's just that…"

Kendall waited as her sister steered the stroller into a department store.

"Well, I've been waiting forever for you to meet the guy who will do exactly what this one has done."

She held her hand up to ward Celia off. "Let's pretend for a minute that what you just said makes sense. Which it doesn't. What has this supposed guy 'done' to me?"

"He's made you speechless."

Kendall stopped in the entryway, blocking the way for others, and stared at her sister open-mouthed.

Celia pointed a finger at her. "Got you."

"WE NEED TO DISCUSS THE progress on the holiday open house."

Troy sat at the dining room table sharing Sunday brunch with the rest of the family, his mind everywhere but on eggs Benedict or the fruit he'd just placed on a side plate, much less the Christmas party the Metaxas hosted at the house every year.

Well, maybe everywhere was an exaggeration. Unless that everywhere led straight to Kendall Banks's long, sexy legs. Essentially where all roads of thought led to ever since he'd given in to temptation and gone to the bed-and-breakfast the other night.

What was he talking about? He'd been distracted ever since meeting her in the diner Wednesday morning.

His cousin Bryna checked her notes. "We still haven't decided on the main item for the gift bags."

"Cookies," Troy said.

Bryna leveled an impatient gaze at him. "We already voted against cookies, remember? Besides, we agreed that Miss Thekla can't possibly be expected to make dozens of cookies between now and then and also cook for everyone as well."

Troy looked at his watch for the fifth time in as many minutes. He hadn't liked the way he'd left Kendall's room Friday night. Thanks to Mrs. Foss, he'd virtually catapulted from the bed, rushing from here to there looking for his clothes, his greatest fear running into the crotchety old woman on his way out. He'd even stubbed his toe against a chair leg.

Kendall had stayed in bed, not bothering to cover her luscious breasts as she'd lain watching him, plainly amused. "Are you sure you want to leave when there's a perfectly good place for you to sleep right here?" she'd asked.

That had caught him up short. Made him realize what an ass he was being. While she was apparently used to men rushing around her bedroom half dressed and half out of their mind, he wasn't.

"I'm sorry," Ari said at his elbow. "Is there somewhere more important you have to be?"

"Actually, there is. I wanted to go to the office to go over those numbers Philippidis faxed through late Friday."

"Even you have to take time out to eat," his father said.

He indicated his plate. "I'm eating."

"So while you're eating, we talk."

He should have known better than to challenge any of his family members over food. Greeks loved their meals. The larger and longer the better. And trying to wiggle out of them was to invite a penalty worse than death.

"Fine," he said. "Where does everything stand on the decorations?"

"The Berman brothers are coming over tomorrow to start work."

"Supervising?"

Ari sipped from his coffee cup. "Frixos."

"Do you think he can handle it? Remember last year they put up red lights instead of clear because Mr. Frixos couldn't tell the difference between the two," Bryna said.

"I don't think it's a mistake they'll be making again," Troy pointed out. "Besides, none of us can spare the time."

"Because?" Bryna asked.

"Because we're going over the contract again tomorrow, section three, paragraphs four, five and nine."

She gave an exaggerated eye roll. "Surely it can't take all day?"

Troy stared at her.

"Fine. Fine."

Ari's fiancée Elena quietly cleared her throat. "I can supervise, if you like. Just give me the work order. If I have any questions, I can always call Ari."

"Or me," Troy's father spoke up.

Everyone looked at him. Interestingly, none of

them had thought of asking him to oversee the work, even though he was the one with the most time on his hands. He'd withdrawn so much as to be little more than a ghost away from the dining table.

"In fact," he said, "why don't I help Elena? I'm sure between the two of us, we'll have this place looking tip-top in no time."

The two shared a smile.

"Buffet," Troy tossed out.

"Who's leading this meeting?" Bryna asked. "You or me?"

Troy made a sweeping gesture. "Be my guest."

His cousin glowered briefly before going into a detailed monologue of those items that they wanted that Miss Thekla said she could make, and others that they would have brought in and handled by the caterers they'd hired for the night.

"Do you have the contract yet?" Troy asked.

"Are you back to business again?" Bryna asked.

"The caterers. Surely there's a contract involved."

"Oh." Bryna looked through her file.

Ari sat back. "They're coming by the office Tuesday with it," he reminded her.

She looked instantly relieved. "Good."

"Of course," Troy said, "you'll want to make sure you read the fine print clearly—"

A collective groan made him grimace.

"Just sayin'."

"Yes, well, you're always just saying." Bryna sighed.

Troy finished off what he could of his eggs and reached for his coffee cup.

Ari smirked. "If we could just get the guy laid, maybe he would lighten up a little."

The coffee cup in Troy's hand slipped and nearly catapulted across the table toward his cousin. Bryna gasped and jumped up, little speckles of black liquid across her white blouse.

"Butterfingers," she said.

His dad handed her his napkin, Elena went off to see if she could scare up a bottle of club soda from Miss Thekla and Ari...

Ari was grinning at Troy as if he, and only he, were in possession of a big, juicy secret.

Troy squinted at him.

"Okay, apparently things are well in hand," he said, getting quickly to his feet. "So you won't mind if I excuse myself."

Silence followed his departure, then Bryna said, "What's up with him?"

His footsteps slowed as he willed his brother to keep his thoughts to himself. "Oh, I don't know. You know Troy. Probably he's having wet dreams about this contract..."

He released a sigh of relief and continued on toward the door and sweet escape.

7

THE FOLLOWING MONDAY afternoon in the Metaxas meeting room, Kendall watched Troy go over the contested contract points with strength and confidence. Damn, but the man was hot.

"Kendall?"

"Hmm?" She looked to Troy's brother, who sat at her right.

"What do you think? Surely Philippidis won't like the revision."

She twisted her lips. "Philippidis never likes anything that isn't to his advantage."

Quiet laughs from around the table.

"I'll advise him of your wishes and get back to you," she said.

She wasn't sure when it had happened, but sometime over the past week she'd come to feel more a part of the team surrounding her than Manolis

Philippidis's. But he was her client. Which meant she was obligated to put him and his interests first.

So far, she'd been given carte blanche, with any inquiries she consulted him about lobbed back at her to handle as she deemed best.

The problem with that was that her loyalties were shifting. And staring at the man responsible for the change like she had just gotten out of his bed and wanted nothing but to jump back into it wasn't going to help matters any.

She cleared her throat. "Now, I do think we need to take a closer look at page thirty-three, Paragraph two..." she directed.

The fact that a man was swaying her emotions during a negotiation didn't bother her as much as it should have. She was coming to recognize that the people around him were as much to credit. His brother Ari was as shrewd as Troy, but willingly sat back when he surged ahead, giving him the front seat without argument, even if his handsome face mirrored his amusement. What was also always there was respect. Not merely from Ari, but from everyone there.

She'd never met Caleb Payne before this. But she'd since done a little snooping within the Philippidis organization and understood that while Caleb had served in a consultant capacity over the years, Manolis had considered him his right-hand man.

Watching Caleb now interact with Troy with enthusiasm and deference spoke volumes.

And the fact that her mind kept traveling back to the other night quite possibly had more than a little to do with it. Talk about hot!

The meeting began to break up. Kendall found herself immediately seeking out Troy's gaze. She hadn't spoken to him since their Friday night activities. And found she wanted to almost desperately. If only to have his full attention on her for a few, uninterrupted moments.

"Okay, everyone, let's break for the day," Troy finally said.

But instead of looking at her, as she'd hoped, he gathered his things together and spoke quietly to his brother, inching his way toward the door.

Kendall scrawled a note on the corner of her pad, tore it from the page and casually got to her feet. Nodding to the others, she walked over to the coffee set up on a table near the door.

"Oh, excuse me," she murmured, working her way between the brothers and brushing ever so slightly against Troy as she did so. She registered his instant expression of surprise and smiled. "I, um, just wanted a bit of coffee while I finish up my notes."

Ari tucked his chin against his chest, not doing a good job of hiding his amusement while Troy failed miserably at disguising his own emotions as he moved quickly back away from her.

She squashed a laugh as she discreetly tucked her note into Troy's jacket pocket and then continued on toward the coffee table.

TROY WALKED TO HIS OFFICE, ignoring the looks his brother gave him as he walked beside him.

"That's one hot woman," Ari commented.

Troy grimaced. "Yes, well, I'm sure Elena would appreciate you saying so."

"I didn't mean for me."

He ducked inside his office. "Since when have you appointed yourself matchmaker?"

Ari prevented him from closing the door. "Since your sad lack of a love life has made you the dark cloud in the room."

His brother squinted at him.

Troy scowled at him, afraid of what he might see if he looked a little too closely. "Don't you have work to do?"

Ari grinned.

Troy shut the door in his face.

He should have smothered him when his parents first brought him home from the hospital.

He walked to his desk and checked his messages. Patience, his secretary, had left early to see to some appointment or another, so whatever questions he had or calls that needed to be made he'd have to see to on his own.

One of the messages was from a supplier who

had directed Patience to write DONE in all capital letters. At any other time, with any other supplier, he might have questioned what it meant. Not here. He knew it meant that his order had been cancelled and there was nothing further to discuss.

Of course, Troy had never learned to take no for an answer.

He put the messages down, his gaze catching on a familiar square of green. He picked up the envelope and turned it over as if it might bite him.

Hadn't he thrown this out?

He sighed, deciding that Patience must have thought the unwanted holiday greetings from his ex-girlfriend and ex-friend had fallen into the garbage can and fished it back out for him.

How thoughtful of her.

He reached around his desk and threw it in the can again. Then drew in a deep breath and took it back out.

Oh, just open it and be over with it already, he ordered himself.

He worked his thumb under the gold seal on the back and then slid the card out. The front featured a black-and-white photograph of downtown Earnest during better times. He opened the card.

"Troy." It was Gail's swirly handwriting. *"Ray and I hope you are doing well. We both miss you and would love to see you. Please accept our calls. Happy Holidays. Love, Gail."*

He stared at the words but they refused to make sense. She wasn't possibly suggesting that bygones by bygones and the three of them should be friends? Not after all that had happened? He didn't care if they had gone on to get married. His best friend had stolen his girl, and she'd gone willingly. As far as he was concerned, that's where the story ended.

He leaned over and threw the card away for a final time and ran his hands over his face. What was the world coming to?

He dragged in a deep breath, his senses instantly filled with Kendall's sweet scent. He stretched his neck and shoved his hands into his jacket pockets, feeling the desire for a nice, long run. Physical activity that would help relieve the tension that had built up between his shoulder blades and appeared to be going nowhere.

His fingers hit the edge of something in his pocket. Frowning, he pulled out a bit of lined yellow paper.

"Meet me at the Hideaway Motel at nine."

Now that was one written request he would be happy to honor…

THE MOTEL WAS A REAL HOLE in the wall a distance from town. Not that Troy didn't already know that. He'd been there on a number of occasions in the past, related mostly to high school activities like homecoming and after-prom parties. But if the squat,

L-shaped twelve-room unit had been bad back then, it was even worse now.

He slowly pulled into the lot, asking himself for the fifth time in as many minutes if he was sure of what he was doing. To have slept with Kendall once was forgivable to a point—how long was a man expected to ignore such a hot invitation?—but going back for seconds...

Well, that negated his argument that what he'd shared with the attractive attorney amounted to a one-night stand. But since he'd never indulged in one before, he wasn't sure what the rules were. Or if there even were rules.

Did a second time a relationship make?

He grimaced, spotting Kendall's red sports car immediately between a twenty-year-old rusty pickup truck he was afraid he recognized and a plain sedan bearing Montana plates.

He parked and killed the engine but didn't immediately get out. It wasn't too late to turn back...

And do what? Torture himself with thoughts of his ex...or exes?

Ever since giving in to the temptation to read the greeting card from Gail and Ray, he'd been mulling over everything in his mind. Revisited memories that he'd thought were long forgotten.

But that didn't matter. There was no forgiveness to be had in this case. He was betrayed. Plain and simple. There was no going back. No changing events that were forever etched in the back of his mind.

And he certainly had no interest in rekindling a friendship with either one of them.

Okay, truth be told, he did miss Ray. But he put it down more to routine than any genuine emotion. Back then he and Ray had been closer than he and Ari had been. They'd run together nearly every morning, enjoyed beer and darts at the pub a couple of nights a week, and had been each other's sounding board.

Then came that one fateful night that changed everything…

Muttering a low curse under his breath, he jerked open the car door and climbed out, scanning the closed windows and doors. Just because her car was parked in front of one room, didn't mean she was in that particular room. Perhaps the truck had already been parked there and she'd taken the spot next to it? The same with the sedan. Hell, he was parked in front of a room and it wasn't his.

The door directly in front of her car opened and she stepped into the doorway, leaning against the jamb and smiling at him suggestively.

Troy knew a moment of hesitation. Not because he was having second thoughts. Rather, he was amazed that the instant Kendall Banks entered the picture, all other thought was wiped from his mind.

She'd removed her suit jacket, but otherwise was

dressed much as she had been earlier at the mill. Her white blouse dipped low between her breasts and her pencil skirt drew his gaze to her narrow waist and her mile-long legs, legs made longer still by the stiletto pumps she had on.

"I wondered if the place scared you away," she murmured as he drew closer.

He looked around him. "It didn't always use to be this bad."

"Oh? Come here a lot?"

He grinned. "Let's just say that I'm…intimate with the place."

She raised a brow, her golden hair a sexy halo around her face.

"When I was back in high school," he admitted.

She smiled and moved from in front of the door. "At least you have memories of better times. Quite honestly, the place nearly scared me away."

Troy closed the door behind him. She'd already drawn the curtains and rather than switching on the TV, she'd turned on the clock radio instead, the tinny sound of a Seattle jazz station filling the room along with occasional static, the result of a weak signal.

She'd stripped the bed of the spread and thrown the patterned navy and green polyester over a chair in the corner. The bed was covered in simple white sheets, the pillows fluffed and laid at odd angles.

"I had to call twice to get them to bring newer

sheets," she said, walking around the other side of the bed.

"I bet."

He was surprised she'd made the effort.

Then he noticed that housekeeping hadn't been the only thing she'd been up to. A bottle of red wine was breathing on a nightstand, two glasses that didn't belong anywhere near this seedy establishment placed next to it. And at least a dozen white candles of all sizes burned on either side of the bed, the only source of light in the room.

And if he wasn't mistaken, fastened to the headboard were two straps.

He walked closer, examining the lengths of leather.

"Two of my belts," she said quietly.

He stared at her.

Her smile looked decidedly devilish. "So are you ready to have the time of your life, Mr. Metaxas?"

8

A THRILL RACED OVER Kendall's skin at the thought of bringing Troy to his knees with pure, sexual need.

She kicked off her shoes, tugged her blouse from the waist of her skirt and then quickly unbuttoned it. He held the free end of one of her belts in his hand, as if unable to believe his eyes.

"You're not afraid, are you?" she asked softly.

He blinked dazedly up at her, his gaze automatically following her movements when she let her blouse fall to the floor, along with her skirt, bra and panties.

He shook his head. "Should I be?"

"Depends."

"On what?" He shrugged out of his suit jacket, laying it across the covered chair, and unbuttoned his shirt.

"On what frightens you."

He stripped his shirt off, and then his trousers, within moments standing in the flickering candle-light sporting nothing but his upright erection. He seemed to remember something and then took out a handful of condoms from his pocket and placed them on the nightstand.

She raised a brow.

He grinned. "Just in case."

She liked the way he thought.

Kendall poured the wine and rounded the bed to hand him a glass.

His dark eyes glinted at her suggestively. "Are you saying I need this?"

She reached down with her free hand, cupping his hard-on. "Mmm…I just thought you might like it."

His eyes grew darker still as his pupils grew large…along with the appendage she held tightly in her palm.

He practically gulped the wine.

It was all she could do not to laugh. "Thirsty?"

"Anxious to see what you have in mind."

She leaned in and kissed him. Long…leisurely… tasting the fruit of the wine on his tongue, the heat of his rising desire on his lips.

"Mmm…"

She placed her hands against his shoulders, moving him to face her, his back to the bed. Then she gently shoved, forcing him to sit.

"Don't worry. I'm not going to whip out an alien

probe," she assured him when he looked slightly panicked.

He raised a brow, amusement showing.

"Unless you want me to…" she teased.

He chuckled. "Go easy on me."

"Oh, easy has absolutely no place in this equation."

"What does?"

She tilted her head slightly as she indicated he should lie down in the middle of the bed. "Let's just say that the other night, you had control…" She climbed up on the mattress after him. "Tonight it's my turn."

She straddled him, watching as his eyes darkened, his gaze taking in her nakedness even as she smoothed her hands along his right side and up his arm, raising it above his head.

"You smell good," she said, and he did. A cross between sandalwood and something spicy. Pepper, maybe.

"It's my cologne."

She fastened the leather around his wrist and he automatically tugged against it, testing it.

"For a minute earlier, I thought Ari might be on to us," she said, trying to keep his mind engaged, off what she was doing in case he balked and wanted to back out.

She realized she needn't worry about that. He was so taken with watching her breasts sway inches away from his mouth while she worked that she could have cracked a whip in front of his nose and he wouldn't have blinked.

"Ari couldn't find his own ass with both hands and a flashlight."

She smiled as she repeated her actions with his other arm, not stopping until use of his arms was no longer an option.

She sat back on his thighs and considered her handiwork. God, there was something infinitely exciting about taking power away from a powerfully hot man.

"I think you underestimate him."

"Hmm…what? Who?"

Kendall was perfectly aware that the way she sat allowed him a special view of her more delicate areas.

"Ari," she said, sliding her hand slowly under her breasts, over her abdomen and then down into the valley between her legs.

Troy's jaw tightened. "Fuck Ari."

She laughed low in her throat as she used her own fingers to spread her damp folds, giving him an even more intimate peek. "No, Troy. I'd much rather fuck you…"

DAMN, BUT THE WOMAN was on fire…

Troy tugged on the straps holding his hands above his head, his palms itching with the desire to caress those beautiful breasts...to probe the flesh between her rounded thighs.

The realization that he couldn't set his teeth on edge as he was instantly relegated to voyeur over participant.

Kendall stroked herself and then smoothed her own juices over the top of his aching hard-on.

He threw his head back and groaned.

He'd heard the term "white-bread" before. As in something mediocre, everyday, mundane. But he'd never truly understood its meaning. Until now. Because everything that had come before this one moment—all his sexual relationships—had been far too white-bread. Predictable. First base, second base, third base, home. Nice. But certainly not thrilling.

Kendall—

She wrapped her fingers around his penis and squeezed. He gasped.

Kendall was feeding a fire within him that he might never have realized he had the fuel for if she'd not entered his life.

She slid her fingers up and down his shaft. He yanked against his restraints.

"Shh..." she murmured.

Then her tongue was on him.

Oh dear Lord in heaven...

Troy's hips bucked from the mattress on their own accord. He set his jaw, warding off his impending crisis. Too quick…too soon. But how was he possibly to have been prepared for this sexy onslaught?

Kendall swirled her tongue around the sensitive head and then slid her lips over to the rim, sucking lightly.

His hips bucked again.

She laughed and removed her mouth. "My, we're the impatient one tonight, aren't we?" She moved her hand up and down, up and down, slowly, tantalizingly… "So different than the other night."

The other night…

The other night he had been the initiator. Had set the pace. Had controlled what happened.

Now he was at her utter, complete mercy.

And she was loving every minute of it.

And, he realized, so was he.

She slid her mouth back over him again, matching her hand movements to her mouth. Troy swallowed thickly, trying to hold back. Attempting to prolong the flames licking through his stomach and around his balls. But he couldn't.

He tried to warn her as his back stiffened.

But she held tight as he exploded into the hot depths of her mouth.

TROY'S OBVIOUS SURPRISE at her actions further heightened Kendall's own desire. She ran her tongue the length of his erection, amazed that he'd lost rigidity for only a moment before going rock hard again. How badly she wanted to feel him deep inside her.

His low groan was more pleasing than the music coming from the small radio. She breathed in his musk, loving the smell of him, the feel, the heat.

Finally, she lapped her way up his defined abs, detouring briefly to suckle his flat nipples, and then kissed him. He leaned up into her, seeking a closer meeting. One she was only too eager to offer him.

So hot…

She wriggled her body against his, enjoying the crisp hair on his chest against her hard nipples, the rasp of his thighs against hers. She wanted his hands on her. Touching her. Stroking her. But in order to achieve that, she'd have to release his bonds. And she wasn't quite ready to do that.

Kendall tore her mouth from his, gasping for air. What was it about this one man that so little could give her so much pleasure?

She slid her legs on either side of his and then straddled him anew. She took one of his condoms from the nightstand and quickly sheathed him, staring deeply into his eyes. Then, inch by delicious inch, she sank down on top of him, taking him in.

A bone-rocking shudder rippled through her, from her scalp to her toes.

As she gazed at him, it struck her why having sex with him was different.

He was there.

Oh, she didn't mean physically. Of course he was there in that regard. No, it went much further than that. He was present. With her. In the moment. No glancing at the clock. No rushing. No evidence of any other place that he'd rather be than with her.

The realization was startling in its clarity. And shot the flames of her desire for him even higher.

She shifted her hips, sliding over him, loving the way he filled her. Touched her.

She rested her palms against his chest, feeling the beat of his heart there. Feeling her own heart beat in synchronicity with his. Feeling connected to him in a way that far transcended sex.

And here she had just been aiming for an incredibly erotic night of sex.

Instead, she'd reached a plateau for which she hadn't been aware she'd been reaching.

She sank down on top of him again and again... oddly both in and out of control. She might be commanding her actions, but she had little if no command over her spiraling, expanding emotions.

Kendall restlessly licked her lips, seeking air that she couldn't seem to draw into her lungs as she leaned over to kiss him. He yanked hard on his restraints. She considered letting him go. Wanted more than anything to feel his arms around her, holding her.

Before she could make the decision, he pulled his right wrist free, tearing the leather, his hand immediately seeking and finding her bottom. He probed her flesh, following her shallow channel down to where they were joined.

Oh, yes...oh, yes...oh, yes...

Then he was holding her ass still, his hips bucking up against hers, filling her deeper, faster. She reached to free his other hand but before she accomplish the task, her body exploded with pleasure, robbing her of any thought outside that of immediate bliss...

9

"YOU SEEM DIFFERENT somehow."

The following day Troy sat in the front booth at the Quality Diner, his father across from him. But it was neither the eatery nor his father that he was contemplating, but rather last night and the hours he'd spent in that motel room with Kendall.

He'd woken this morning surprised to find himself still in bed with her, yet reluctant to get out of it. To move her leg from where it lay across his. To put an end to her soft snores where her head rested against his shoulder.

He'd lain there, caressing her back with his hand, marveling at the soft warmth of her skin, the sweet smell of her blond hair, thinking that for the first time in a long time, he felt at peace.

He frowned now, finding his choice of description odd. To feel peace meant that one was at war, no?

If so, what was he at war with? And how did he go about ending it permanently?

He finally focused on his father and his question. "I'm sorry. What was that?"

His father appeared not to know whether to grin or frown. "You're distracted."

Troy picked up the menu. "I'm not distracted. I'm preoccupied. I'd like to get this contract sewn up before Philippidis changes his mind."

His father took the menu from his hands. "You're distracted. We already ordered."

Had they? God, he couldn't even remember.

Which made him all the more curious about his state of mind.

He'd never been so out of sorts over a woman before. Or if he had, he couldn't remember it. Which could very possibly be the case, considering that he couldn't even remember ordering.

He stopped short of asking his father what he would be eating for breakfast, however.

"What were we talking about?" he prompted his father.

"Your distractedness."

"Before that."

"The fact that Elena bought half of this diner."

Troy nodded and looked around. "Ah, yes. And she hasn't broken the news to Ari yet."

His brother was going to be upset that his bride-to-be had gone against his wishes. But from what he understood, Elena's actions were good for everyone involved. She could have bought Verna out completely considering that the longtime owner was suffocating under a mountain of debt. Instead, Elena had bought half interest, providing the capital Verna needed to dig herself out, yet hold on to the place her family had established over a hundred years ago. And from what he could tell, the two women got along like a house on fire. Even now, he could see both of them through the kitchen window laughing as they cooked together.

His gaze homed in on Elena's beautiful face. Okay, he reluctantly admitted, maybe he'd been wrong about her. Perhaps she hadn't been marrying Philippidis for his money and wasn't the gold digger he'd thought. In fact, he was growing quite fond of her and her strong independent streak. Lord knew it would be much easier for her just to go along with Ari's wishes. Money was not in short supply and she would be well taken care of. That she wanted to make her own way, and was slowly integrating herself with the town inhabitants, all while her belly grew larger each passing day, was endearing.

"He's not going to take the news well," his father said of Ari.

"He'll get over it."

"I suppose he will. I think he'll feel better once Elena finally agrees on a wedding date. I mean, that baby she's carrying isn't getting any smaller."

Troy grinned at his father's traditional views. "She'll agree when she's ready."

"In the meantime we have to put up with Ari."

Which wasn't a bad proposition. Of the two of them, his younger brother had always been the one with the better disposition. Of course, with him around to look after the more important matters, what was there for Ari to worry about?

"Then there's the other matter," Percy said quietly.

Troy squinted at him as the waitress brought them their lunches. He was relieved he'd gone with a club salad and not half a grapefruit or something else equally as unappetizing from the menu.

"Where did you stay last night?"

Troy nearly choked on his own saliva. "I came home."

His father narrowed his eyes.

"Would you believe me if I told you I slept on the couch in my office at the mill?"

"If it's the truth."

He'd never liked lies. Not even little white ones.

But in this case he figured he was entitled. He could only imagine what his father would do with the news that he'd slept with opposing council.

"Is it?" Percy asked.

The cowbell above the door opened. He was surprised to see Caleb enter along with a handsome, well-dressed older woman.

Troy wiped his mouth with his napkin and got to his feet. "Caleb." He nodded at the other man.

His father followed suit, but his gaze wasn't on his niece's boyfriend. Instead, he appeared quite taken with the woman.

After Caleb greeted them both, he put his arm around her and said, "May I present my mother, Phoebe Payne."

Troy welcomed her to Earnest and inquired if she was enjoying her visit. His father kissed her hand and offered to show her around.

Troy knew a moment of pause, dread coating the bottom of his stomach. They suspected part of the reason Manolis Philippidis had decided to let bygones be bygones was because he hoped to win back Phoebe Payne, who he had been dating until she'd learned of his bullish behavior.

What was his father doing?

Caleb said, "A word, Troy?"

He followed when Caleb stepped a few feet away.

"I have that meeting with the union head this afternoon. Can you pop in? Kind of a feel-good gesture? I have a feeling that this isn't going to go as smoothly as we hoped."

"Why? What's happened?"

"There's some concern over job guarantees."

Troy rubbed the back of his neck. "Seeing as there

are no jobs to be had anywhere in Earnest, I'd think they'd be a little more amenable."

Caleb grimaced. "Not a point you want to make. I already tried that and the brick wall raised higher."

"Okay. Fine. What time?"

"We're meeting at two-thirty, so fifteen minutes or so thereafter would be good."

He nodded. "Fine. Good." He turned to find his father had led Phoebe to their booth and was handing her in to sit next to him.

Christ. This was a disaster waiting to happen.

Caleb grinned. "Looks like we'll be dining together."

"Yes. Looks that way," Troy said under his breath.

And if the only things on his father's menu were food, everything would be great...

AFTER THE FIRST FEW DAYS of working inside the main conference room, Troy had offered Kendall use of an empty office at the mill just down the way from his. She'd thankfully accepted and spent most of her time in the airy space going over her notes, communicating with Philippidis's office and punching numbers into her laptop.

Movement outside caught her attention. She didn't realize she was hoping it was Troy until she experienced disappointment at discovering it wasn't.

"Have you even had lunch?" Bryna asked, leaning against the doorjamb.

She lifted a carton of chocolate milk. "I'm brown-bagging it, compliments of Mrs. Foss."

"Really?"

Curiosity brought Troy's younger cousin closer to peek at what was left of her lunch.

She chuckled. "Peanut butter and jelly?"

"Along with a bag of chips and an apple."

"God, how old does she think you are?"

"Not too old that I didn't enjoy it. She even cut off the crust. My mother never even did that."

They enjoyed a shared laugh as Kendall finished off her milk and tossed the carton along with the other wrappings into the wastebasket.

She liked Bryna. She was smart and open and didn't pull any punches. Qualities that seemed to run in the Metaxas family. Once or twice she'd caught her and Caleb Payne sneaking a kiss in the semi-privacy of Bryna's office, but while it was obvious the two were dating, they were discreet about it.

Of course, during the long contract meetings for which they were all present, Kendall had a hard enough time making sure she wasn't too obviously mooning over Troy to pay much attention to anyone else.

"So tell me," she said casually. Or at least she hoped she sounded casual. "Are all of you Metaxases involved in relationships?"

"Involved?"

"You and Caleb…"

"Oh!" Her cheeks colored briefly and her smile was so wide it nearly split her pretty face in two. "You noticed."

"I noticed."

"It isn't too obvious, I hope? I don't think Troy would be too happy about any workplace displays of affection."

"No, nothing obvious…outside the fact that you two have the hots for each other big-time."

Bryna looked down at her hands, her expression revealing that she was probably thinking thoughts she wouldn't share.

"And Ari is engaged to Elena at the diner."

Bryna gave an exaggerated eye roll. "I swear, if they don't get married soon, their child will be able to stand up for them at the wedding."

"Is there a specific reason for the delay?"

"I think Elena wants everyone to be clear that she's not marrying him for his money. Until she feels comfortable that's the case…"

"I see." She paused. "And Troy?"

"Troy?"

Kendall was afraid she was caught.

"Are you kidding? Troy hasn't had a date in something like two years."

Kendall might have given a sigh of relief had she not been shocked by the answer. "Two years?"

Bryna nodded. "Yep. Not since his ex-girlfriend went off and married his best friend."

She winced. "Ouch."

"You can say that again. Nasty business."

It was, indeed. Kendall couldn't imagine what Troy must have gone through. It was bad enough losing your girl to another man, but to have that man be your best friend... She shuddered.

She reached inside the plain brown bag and pulled out a baggy. "Mrs. Foss included a few homemade oatmeal cookies. Want one?"

Bryna groaned as she sat on a corner of the desk. "I'd love one. I haven't had oatmeal cookies since... well, since I last had a pb&j sandwich." She accepted a cookie. "Miss Thekla doesn't make them."

"Miss Thekla?"

"Our housekeeper."

Neither of them said anything more as they polished off the three cookies, Kendall offering up half of the third and Bryna happily taking it off her hands.

"Is a packed lunch included in the daily rate?" Bryna asked.

Kendall smiled. "I asked Mrs. Foss if she'd mind me making a sandwich to take for lunch using leftovers one night, and from there on in I found a brown bag waiting for me next to my breakfast plate. So, yes, I guess it is included."

"Maybe she's softening up in her old age."

Kendall laughed. "I wouldn't go that far."

Movement on the catwalk. They both turned to watch Troy and Caleb return from their own lunch, deep in conversation.

"Uh-oh," Bryna said, getting to her feet and brushing cookie crumbs from her skirt. "I'd better get back to my office before the boss discovers I'm missing and docks my pay."

"I'm sure you'd never let that happen."

"You're right." She paused at the door. "You are going to make the Christmas party, aren't you?"

"Party?"

"You mean Troy hasn't invited you yet?"

Indeed, he hadn't. "An office event?"

"More like a whole town event. The family's been doing it for decades. We host an open house for the entire town. Food, drink, music, gifts…the whole shebang. It's this Saturday night. I'm sure Troy just forgot. I don't know if you've noticed, but he's a little work obsessed."

"I've noticed."

"Anyway, I'm inviting you. So please come."

Kendall knew a moment of pause, momentarily wondering if Troy had, indeed, forgotten to invite her. Or whether he just didn't want her there. "Thanks. I'll think about it."

"Good." She turned back toward the door. "Thanks for the cookie."

"Anytime."

10

LATER THAT NIGHT, KENDALL sat on her bed at the B and B, pillows propped up behind her, trying to focus on the revisions in the contract in front of her. She picked up her cell phone from the bedding and checked the display, but it showed her nothing more than it had half a minute ago. Namely, that Troy hadn't tried to contact her.

It was just after nine and she was beginning to think that perhaps she had come on a little too strong at the motel. Had she freaked him out? Made him wonder what she had in mind for next time?

She put the torturously quiet cell phone back down and turned the page of the contract, making another notation in the margin. It was storming outside, insulating her further from the world around her. Something scratched against the window and she looked in that direction. Probably a tree branch blowing in the wind.

She sighed.

Whereas Troy seemed completely capable of forgetting about her, she couldn't seem to stop thinking about him.

Of course, it didn't help that she was sitting on a bed in which they'd had some of that hot sex she wanted more of. But it wasn't just the sex. More and more she found herself wondering about things that had nothing to do with his chiseled body and more about his psychological makeup. What had he been like as a child? Had he always been so serious? The boy on the Little League team with the determined grimace just waiting for his turn to knock the ball out of the park? The kid with the route who delivered his papers five minutes after they were distributed to him? The cute Cub Scout that appeared at your door outlining how many more candy bars he had to sell to earn his next merit patch and refused to let you go back inside until you bought something?

She smiled and snuggled down a little further into the pillows. There was something immensely satisfying about getting him to act outside his comfort zone. She merely had to think of him with his hands bound above his head to get hot all over again.

Had he ever intentionally taken a walk in the rain? Or called in sick when he wasn't?

Her gaze drifted from the contract pages to the silent cell phone again. She reached out to pick it up, and jumped when it rang in her hand.

She hurried to answer without looking at the display.

"Hello?"

"Kendall?"

Troy. She sighed against the pillows. "Are you looking for someone else?"

"What? Who…oh." His warm chuckle filled her ear and shivered all over. "Hi."

"Hi, yourself."

If she felt a little too happy about hearing from him, she wasn't going to acknowledge the fact. At least not to herself. Right now, it was better just to feel. So what if the mere sound of his voice made her squeeze her thighs together? Chased away the damp chilliness of the day?

"What are you doing?" he asked.

"Mmm…nothing much. How about you?"

"Same here."

Kendall moved the contract from her lap to the nightstand and curved against the pillows. "Did you call for some phone sex?"

"Phone…er. No."

She made a face.

"What was that?" he asked.

The same ting she'd heard earlier sounded against the window. "What was what?"

"That sound?"

Another *ting,* this time louder.

Kendall got up from the bed and stepped barefoot to the window.

Standing below it in the rain was none other than Troy.

"I thought you'd never look out," he said.

She put her hand over her mouth to muffle her laugh. "What are you doing?"

"Trying to get your attention, of course."

"You could have rung the bell."

"Not without getting Mrs. Foss's attention."

"You could have called."

"Isn't that what I'm doing?"

Another voice sounded. Kendall leaned her forehead against the window, watching as Mrs. Foss appeared through the back door. What was that in her hand? A broom?

Kendall gasped as the old woman landed a solid whack against the back of Troy's legs.

"I gotta go," he said into the phone. "Meet me around the side on Maple. I'll be waiting..."

He hung up.

She stayed at the window for a long moment, watching as he ran toward the street, Mrs. Foss shaking her broom after him.

The old woman looked up. Kendall moved quickly away from the window, laughing harder than she'd laughed in a good long time...

TROY SHRUGGED OUT OF HIS soaked suit jacket and hung it on the back of his leather car seat, then ran his hands through his dripping hair. He'd never done anything so spontaneous in his life. Of course, it would serve him right if he was made to pay for it with a nasty cold. He grinned. But it had been so worth it if just to see Kendall's beautiful face peering at him through the window.

It seemed like a good idea at the time. Then the skies had opened up and he'd been caught standing there on the Fosses' lawn, a major target. He could only hope that the rain had spotted Mrs. Foss's glasses enough to make him little more than a blurry mass. He figured it was a good sign that she hadn't addressed him by name. Merely shouted something about no good teenagers today and walloped him with her broomstick. He could still feel the sting across the back of his legs.

The passenger's door opened and Kendall slid onto the passenger's seat next to him.

In that one moment, he knew his questionable actions had been worth it.

"Did you actually throw stones at my window?" she asked.

"I did."

"That's the most romantic thing anyone's ever done for me. Corniest, but romantic."

"I'll take romantic."

Her smile warmed him despite his damp clothes.

She settled in more comfortably against the seat. "So where are we going?"

Now that was a question he didn't have an answer to. "The motel is full." He'd driven by on his way here to see the No Vacancy sign flashing, a neat row of motorcycles parked one after another in the parking lot. Apparently a club had stopped there for the night when the rain had started.

"Of what?"

"Of motorcycle riders."

Her smile turned decidedly naughty. "Sounds kinky."

"Sounds out of bounds."

She laughed and he started the car.

He didn't dare take her back to the Metaxas estate. Not with the open house preparations in full swing. Not only was Elena there with Ari, so was her mother. And Caleb was actually staying over for the first time in a guest room, although not even Percy was naïve enough to think that would hold.

"We could always sneak back up to my room," Kendall suggested.

"And have to worry about being quiet." He shook his head. "No thank you. I've already suffered Mrs. Foss's wrath enough for one day."

He pulled away from the curve as she pushed up the console between their two seats and scooted closer to him.

"Mmm…this is nice."

He curved his arm around her shoulders, agreeing with her assessment. This was, indeed, nice. Very nice. She smelled of warm peaches and toothpaste. All he wanted to do was run his tongue along her smooth teeth.

"You're soaked," she commented, running her hand over the front of his shirt.

"My jacket caught the brunt of it."

She reached up and tousled his wet hair and then reached for the dash controls, turning up the heat and aiming the blowers at him. He was instantly glad for the attention as she ran her fingers through his hair slowly, tantalizingly.

He hadn't had a girl cuddle up to his side while he was driving since he was a teen. He wondered why that was. Could it be because once you were older, and had unfettered access to a bedroom, car canoodling was no longer necessary?

The question presented him with a solution their problem.

"Makeout Cove," he said aloud.

"Makeout what?"

He grinned at where she was popping the buttons on his shirt. "Makeout Cove. It's a place I used to go when I was a younger."

"By yourself or with others?"

"You're being facetious."

"I'm being facetious."

He rubbed his hand down over her shoulder to her arm and back again. Damn, but she was sexier than any woman had a right to be.

He pointed the car in the direction of his destination, glad for the rain for more than privacy issues. Last summer, the area had experienced as close to a drought as they'd ever gotten. Add in an unusual heat wave and the combination had left Earnest and the surrounding counties ripe for mudslides. Just this morning he'd heard on the radio that one had blocked access to Route 6 for three hours while bulldozers cleared the road and rescued a woman trapped in her sedan when the slide hit.

After a few minutes, he reached Makeout Cove and pulled down the long, gravel road toward the dead end many Earnest residents knew intimately. His headlights bounced along the uneven ground, illuminating the overgrown trees whose limbs were weighed down further with tonight's rain.

He'd expected the area to be deserted. Instead, he found two other cars parked, their windows steamed over. He pulled into a spot away from them and put the gear in Park, leaving the engine on to provide heat against the chilly night.

"This is Makeout Cove?" Kendall asked.

"You were expecting something different?"

"A view, maybe?"

Troy ran the back of his knuckles over her cheekbone, brushing her hair back. "The purpose of a place like this is the person you're with is all the view you need."

Her eyes darkened in the amber glow from the

dashboard lights as her gaze shifted from his eyes to his mouth and then back again.

"I feel like I'm fifteen," she whispered. "First the stones against the window—"

"That took a cell phone call for you to respond to."

"Never mind that." She looked around. "Now Makeout Cove." She leaned her forehead against his and whispered, "Can we go for ice cream afterward?"

"Only if you want to."

He leaned in, taking a lingering taste of her lips. She smiled. "I want to."

"I figured you might."

She finished unbuttoning his shirt even as she kicked off her shoes and straddled his hips. She freed him of the damp fabric and asked, "Where's the button to push the seat back?"

He blindly found it, her fragrant hair brushing against the side of his face as she kissed him.

"God, this is so incredibly hot," she murmured, pushing her skirt up so that he glimpsed her panties. She pressed herself against his hard-on and he stretched his neck back, suppressing a groan.

He'd never ached for a woman physically to this almost painful degree before. He slid his fingers up the hem of her skirt and grasped her hips, holding her still even as she fumbled with the catch on his belt.

Were they really going to have sex in his car at Makeout Cove?

She reached inside his pants and took his pulsing length in her hand. He swallowed thickly.

Yes, they were....

_11_

HAD IT ONLY BEEN A SHORT time ago that she'd thought Troy lacking in spontaneity? Had pictured him as an unadventurous youth given to serious grimaces rather than toothy grins?

As Kendall settled her bare flesh against his, she was happy to stand corrected.

For the first time she became aware that a CD played at low volume. Was that Muddy Waters? It seemed Troy was surprising her around every corner tonight.

And as he directed her hips so he could enter her, edging her down until he filled her to the hilt, she found herself wanting him to surprise her even more.

He pressed his thumbs against her clit and she nearly burst right then and there, so unexpected was the move, so sensual.

She shifted her hips forward and then back even

as she framed his striking face in her hands and leaned in to kiss him. His hair was ink black in the dim light, his features in shadow. His breathing was shallow, his skin smelled of rain and limes and tasted of sin as she ran her tongue the length of his jawline and then welcomed his insistent kiss.

His hips bucked upward, filling her again. She stretched her head back, bearing her breasts to him, bracing herself against him with her hands on his thighs. He cursed under his breath and then caught a swollen nipple in his mouth, suckling deeply. Kendall cried out, a red-hot heat swirling within her from multiple directions, leaving her control in strained tatters.

Yes…oh, yes.

There had been so few men who satisfied her to the extent that Troy did…again and again and again. She kept waiting to be disappointed. To kiss him and have the heat no longer there. To feel his hard arousal pressed against her soft flesh and not be moved.

Instead, her need for him increased rather than decreased.

And he appeared to take special pleasure in bringing her to climax, strumming her body like a well-played instrument, plucking and sliding and urging.

Each of his upward thrusts sent her senses soaring, her internal thermometer rising. She squeezed her thighs against his hips, trying to hold off, yearning to prolong the sensations merely having him inside her brought.

But Troy allowed her no quarter. His hands grasped, his hips moved and before she knew what hit her, Kendall was hurtling headfirst into a deliciously wet orgasm....

SOME TIME LATER, KENDALL lay sprawled in the passenger seat, out of breath and covered in a thin sheen of sweat. Outside, the rain continued to pound the car, rivulets running down the steamed windows. Inside, it was warm and cozy.

"Wow..."

Beyond her wildest imaginings, sex with Troy kept getting better and better. Yes, she admitted, it could be the unusual setting. Getting it on in a car had made her feel like a rebellious teenager out past curfew. But somehow that explanation didn't hit the mark. She suspected the reason for her heightening need for Troy Metaxas lay in a place she had yet to explore. And, frankly, was more than a little afraid to.

"So, tell me about this holiday open house."

The words were out of her mouth before she realized she was going to say them.

She froze, cursing inwardly at herself. Where had that come from? And how, exactly, did she go about snatching the words back from midair?

She chanced a glance at Troy. Thankfully, he

didn't appear to find anything curious about the question as he tucked his shirt into his slacks, knocking his knee against the steering wheel in the process.

She, on the other hand, was shocked. By both the query and the motivation behind it.

Yes, she admitted to herself, she'd been a little upset when Bryna had told her about the party. A party Troy had not mentioned to her, much less invited her to attend.

That was unusual enough in and of itself. She usually accepted circumstances at face value. So he hadn't asked her to come. That shouldn't be surprising. They weren't officially dating. She understood that. Moreover, she'd initiated the purely sexual nature of their relationship.

Why, then, was she suddenly feeling like the slighted girlfriend?

Yikes!

She lifted her hand to do up her blouse. "Forget I asked that."

If Troy hadn't been suspicious before, he was now. "Why?"

Kendall bit her bottom lip. This wasn't happening. "Because it's not any of my business."

"Philippidis didn't pass on that you're both invited?"

That should have made her feel better. But it didn't.

"You're upset."

She sighed and then ultimately nodded. Okay, so she wasn't happy with herself and her reaction. But she'd never pulled a punch before. Why start now? So this was unfamiliar territory. She'd figure it out as she went along.

"I'm…disappointed," she admitted.

He squinted at her in the dim light. He'd finished putting himself back together and looked painfully, handsomely disheveled. To her chagrin, she wanted to climb on top of him all over again.

"I don't understand," he said.

She straightened her skirt. "That makes two of us."

He remained silent.

She had hoped by putting her feelings out there, the pocket of unexplainable emptiness that filled her chest would dissipate. Instead, it appeared to grow larger, pressing on her from the inside out.

"I know," she whispered. "It makes no sense. I mean, what did I expect? An engraved invitation?"

"That's so not what this party is about—"

"You don't have to explain," she interrupted. "I'm not even entitled to one."

"Will you let me finish?"

She snapped her mouth shut.

"What I meant is that this open house is exactly that—an open house. My family's been hosting the event for decades. Everyone in Earnest takes part.

No invitations are issued. It's generally understood that anyone who comes is welcome."

"That's nice." A little too much sarcasm? She mentally cringed. Where was all this emanating from? He'd just told her without telling her that she was invited. Welcome.

Perhaps it was his generalization that stung.

Everyone was welcome. Including her. Not her particularly.

"Oh, this is just stupid," she muttered more to herself than him. "Can you just take me back to the B and B, please? Where I can see to screwing my head back on properly."

She stared resolutely through the windshield. A pair of red taillights indicated that one of their fellow cove visitors had finished and were on their way back home.

Troy reached a hand out, fingering a tendril of her hair that was pasted against her cheek. "Are you all right?"

She brushed the hair back and pushed his hand away in the process. Something she hadn't meant to do, but now that it was done….

"I'm fine. Everything's perfect."

No, it wasn't. Who was she kidding? Suddenly it seemed as if everything was far from being okay.

She shifted in her seat to face him more fully.

"What am I to you, Troy?" she asked point-blank.

She suspected that he couldn't have looked more shocked had she just told him he fell well short in the lover area.

"What…?"

Was it the closeness of the holidays? she wondered. Was that why she was getting all sentimental? But she'd never been the mushy type outside of her immediate family.

Perhaps it was because the official signing of the contract was set for tomorrow. Meaning that she would no longer have a reason to see Troy every day. Or at all. Indeed, her presence would no longer be required in town. She'd go back to Portland and… and what?

"Am I even someone you'd consider dating?" she asked.

He blinked, appearing not to know how to respond. Which bothered her even more.

"Oh, just forget it. Take me back now, please."

"What's going on here, Kendall?" he asked softly. "You're not even giving me a chance to answer your questions."

She stared at him, ridiculously close to tears.

What was the matter with her?

"Is this about tomorrow?" he asked. "About the termination of our business arrangement?"

"Excuse me, but I think that's asking questions of your own, not answering mine."

A ghost of a smile. "You're right." He cleared

his throat. "Would I consider dating you?" he repeated. "I consider this...our relationship...beyond
dating..."

"Beyond dating how?"

"Beyond dating in that what I feel for you goes
beyond 'I'd like to take you out to dinner.'"

"And where do you feel this?"

His brows rose high on his forehead. And then he
chuckled as if caught off guard.

"Where?" He shifted uncomfortably.

She leaned over, cupping his manhood in her
hand. "Is this where?"

He groaned and despite her best efforts, Kendall
experienced a renewed desire to cradle him between
her thighs.

"This minute? Yes, there."

She moved to jerk her hand back. He caught it,
staring deep into her face. "But I also feel it here."

He budged her hand upward until it rested against
his chest.

The empty space within Kendall filled with sun-
shinelike warmth.

A brisk knocking on the driver's side window
caused them both to jump.

She pulled her hand back and watched as Troy
pushed the button to lower the window. Standing next
to the car was what appeared to be the same sheriff
who had given her a speeding ticket the week before.

He had on a plastic protected hat, the rain running from the front brim as he considered them.

"Troy," he said.

"Barnaby."

"May I ask what you're doing here this late?"

Kendall felt the irrepressible desire to laugh.

"Oh," Troy said, looking to her and then back at the sheriff. "I'd say we're doing what other couples do. We're sitting here watching the rain."

"Uh-huh." Barnaby shined his flashlight inside the car and onto Kendall. "The rain."

"Are you going to charge us with something, Barnaby?" Troy asked.

"I could ticket you for public indecency."

"But you didn't catch us in the act."

He shined the light in Troy's face. "I have the feeling that if I got here five minutes ago, I would have."

Kendall did laugh, quickly lifting her hand to her mouth to muffle the sound.

The flashlight flicked off and the sheriff straightened. "It's raining everywhere, so why don't you enjoy it back in town?"

"Yes, Sheriff," Kendall said. "Thank you."

The tall, good-looking law enforcement officer shook his head and walked back toward his car.

She and Troy enjoyed a laugh as he rolled up the window and put the car in gear.

"I can't believe we got caught," he said, following the sheriff's taillights out of the cove.

"I don't think that really qualifies as getting caught," Kendall said quietly. "I think full coital is the only thing that meets that criteria."

He glanced at her with a grin. "Or really great oral sex."

She smiled, looked at the sheriff's car in front of them, then down at where Troy's erection tented the material of his slacks....

12

THE FOLLOWING MORNING, Kendall considered her reflection in the mirror of her private bathroom at the B and B. She took a deep breath, wondering if the navy blue suit was a little severe. But it was still raining and anything lighter would show every drop. She straightened her wraparound white blouse and wriggled her shoulders to get it to fall right, then sighed.

She seemed to be doing a lot of that since Troy had dropped her off last night.

"You should be happy," she told herself, checking her eyeliner. "The negotiations are coming to a successful close. You've done your job and then some. Every reason to feel good."

Then why didn't she?

Because you won't have an excuse to watch Troy's magnificent ass in his tailored business suits anymore.

She grimaced and went back into the other room. She couldn't decide whether she should stay for the open house tomorrow or not, so she'd half-packed her things, figuring she'd see how she felt at day's end. If everything went well—and she had every expectation that it would—then she'd stay. If not...

She wasn't exactly sure how things might not go well. But she was nothing if not cautious. She always looked both ways before crossing even a quiet street. Locked her windows at night. And when it came to business, she waited until the ink was dry before declaring a contract signed. It was just the way she operated.

Of course, business really didn't have anything to do with her uneasy thoughts. She wanted to see what was going to happen between her and Troy before she decided whether to stay or go. Nothing more. Nothing less.

She opened the last drawer she had to clear out and then closed it again, leaving the undergarments there.

On the bed, her cell phone rang.

She picked it up.

"Good morning," an accented voice greeted.

"Mr. Philippidis," she said with a smile. "I was just leaving now to drive to the mill. Will you be there?"

Silence.

Kendall experienced a moment of dread, afraid of what was to come…

TROY WAS IN THE MIDDLE of one call, had another on hold, and accepted yet another message from Patience, who was aptly named because she had proven time and again that she had an abundance of it.

He listened as the supplier complained about a returned check even as he curved his hand over the mouthpiece to prevent the caller from hearing him. "I hate Fridays," he muttered.

His secretary smiled. "That, my dear Mr. Metaxas, would make you the only one. Everyone else lives for the day. Myself included."

"That's because you don't have to deal with every disaster that's destined to happen."

She waved a sheath of bills. "Don't I?"

She put the papers in his in-box as he turned toward the window and spoke into the mouthpiece. "I understand. And I apologize. Of course, we'll cover the associated charges…"

He took the receiver from his ear. "Patience, be a dear and tell the other line I'll have to call them back."

"Oh, no. You've been putting Mr. Simpson on the back burner all week."

"Invite him to the open house tomorrow."

"All the way from Connecticut? I don't think so."

"Maybe he has family in the area that might like to come."

She gave him a long look and then walked toward the door. "You owe me one."

"I owe you more than that."

"Yes, well, just remember that when you're reviewing salaries next week."

Next week.

He finished up the conversation and then hung up the phone, standing there for a long moment. Just think, this was the last time he was going to have to apologize for a bounced check. Deal with an unhappy supplier. Take lip from his longtime secretary.

Okay, maybe the last one was asking for too much. But he could dream, couldn't he?

He looked at his watch. Only a few more minutes to go. A glance at the conference room told him almost everyone was already there. Almost.

Movement outside his door. He knew an instant of lightness.

Kendall.

He raised his hand to wave at her, only she wasn't looking his way. Not only that but she appeared a little too serious for today's upbeat event.

He frowned, hoping that she hadn't folded in on herself as she had last night in the car.

He gathered his papers together, wondering if he'd ever understand the complicated nature of a woman's heart...

"Woo-hoo!" Ari popped the bottle of champagne he'd brought to celebrate the official signing of the contract and the conference room erupted into cheers, everyone in the surrounding offices coming in to join them in the celebration.

The only one who didn't look happy was Kendall.

Troy looked up from where he'd penned the final flourish, having initialed or signed every page in the one-hundred-and-ten page contract and then closing the document with a satisfied whoosh. He placed a hand on top, reveling in the feeling for a moment. This bit of processed wood pulp and ink represented so much to him, his family and the town of Earnest. The end of hardship. The beginning of revitalization. Upon receipt of the final contract bearing Philippidis's signature, along with his wire transfer of working capital, they could move forward with plans over a year in the making.

He accepted handshakes, man-hugs and back pats from everyone in the room…with the exception of Kendall.

Ari was pouring the champagne into paper cups and handing them out to employees. Patience even rolled in a congratulatory cake he hadn't known she'd ordered.

To his surprise, he found Kendall putting the two copies of the contract that she would personally take to Philippidis for final signatures into her briefcase, and snapping it shut, her face drawn and pale. She didn't raise her gaze as she made her way toward the door.

Troy quickly slid in her direction and blocked her way before she slipped out of the room.

"Where do you think you're going?" he asked with a smile.

He felt like a heavy boulder had been lifted from his shoulders. As if the sun had come out to shine after a too long absence. And he couldn't think of anyone he'd like to celebrate with more than Kendall.

But unless he was reading her wrong, the pinched look on her face said that she wanted to be anywhere else but there.

"I'm needed back home," she said.

He grasped her arm when she tried to maneuver her way around him. "Is everything all right? Your parents? Your sister? Nothing's happened?"

"What? Oh. No." She shook her head. "It's not that kind of need."

"Then what kind is it?"

She stared at him for a long moment, then looked down at her where she tightly held her briefcase.

"You know," Troy began, taking in the soft curve of her lips, the shape of her calves. "Now that business is no longer involved, we can take this public."

"Oh?" she asked quietly. "What do you propose

we do, Troy? Shall I move into the B and B? Or will you be coming to visit me down in Portland?"

He drew back, surprised.

"What, no champagne?" Ari asked, coming up and handing his brother a paper cup, and holding out another to Kendall.

Troy wondered if she'd take it.

She did, barely sipped from it, and then handed it back. "Congratulations. Now if you'll excuse me…"

Troy handed his cup back to his startled brother as well, and followed Kendall out.

"Hey, wait."

She stopped but didn't turn around.

"Is that it, then? You're just going to leave?"

"There's no more business here to discuss. I'll get these contracts to Philippidis, and the finalized version will be forwarded to you next week along with the agreed-upon capital."

He rounded to stand in front of her. "I want you to stay."

"I can't."

"Fine. If you don't want in on today's celebration, at least come to the open house tomorrow."

She caught her bottom lip between her teeth.

"Please. I'd really like to have you there."

"Why?"

He leaned in closer to her, touching the side of her face. "Do you really need to ask?"

She fell silent.

"I want you there because I...like being around you. Because I feel better than when I'm without you." She didn't respond. "Because I'd like to see where this takes us."

"Let me save you the suspense—the bedroom."

He chuckled. "Beyond that."

She seemed to soften slightly.

"Say you'll think about it?"

She looked down at the front of her blouse.

"It wouldn't be the same for me without you there."

"I... We'll see," she whispered. "Now, please, Troy. I've really got to go."

Troy reluctantly stepped aside and watched in helpless confusion as she hurried down the hall as if the devil himself snapped at her heels.

WHAT TROY COULDN'T have known was that the devil had already taken a large chunk out of her. And Kendall was afraid she would spend a lifetime trying to earn back the missing piece.

She returned to the B and B, determined to pack and head home. Now. But once she reached her room, she was out of breath and a little too shaky to consider driving across the street, much less the one hundred and forty miles to Portland.

She collapsed against the door and then slid down the wood to sit on the floor next to her briefcase.

She couldn't believe she'd done it. Couldn't convince herself that what had just happened was real. She prided herself on being tough but honest.

Now she was neither.

Her cell phone rang from the side pocket of her briefcase. It might as well have been a mile away for all the impact it had on her. She merely sat staring straight ahead at nothing, at everything, trying to get control over her breathing.

Thankfully, the phone went silent.

So many images screamed through her mind. Troy's surprised face mere minutes ago. Ari popping the champagne cork. Her father sitting behind his desk. Her sister holding her children.

She lifted her hands to the sides of her head, wishing there were a button somewhere to make it all cease. To stop her brain from reminding her what she'd done that bothered her so. And repeating why it was so despicable that she had.

The cell rang again.

Troy?

Possible, but not probable. He was likely still back at the mill celebrating his great victory.

Or what should have been one.

Kendall blindly searched her case for the damn chirping bit of technology and answered.

"Is it done?"

She cringed at the familiar sound of Manolis Philippidis's voice. "It's done."

She could almost hear him smiling. "Good. Very good. You will be well rewarded for your excellent service."

Kendall stared sightlessly at the cell phone and then dropped it without saying goodbye.

Rewarded...excellent service...

She hadn't done it for either reason. She'd done it to save her father. To prevent Philippidis from closing his company and cutting off his livelihood and hopes of one day buying the place back.

In order to save her family, she'd had to screw Troy's by altering an important page in the contract he'd just signed. One line that gave the wealthy Greek fifty-one percent of Metaxas, Inc. A number that put him in control.

Control he planned to use to shut down the Metaxas brothers. For good this time, because there was a "do not compete" clause that would prevent them from making so much as a bagel if Manolis decided that's what he wanted to do.

An airtight clause that she had worked out.

Troy had believed it was there to protect him.

He hadn't realized it could also be used against him.

She now understood why she'd been asked to close this deal. Now saw why Philippidis had sent her, a virtual outsider, someone who didn't work directly

for his company, in to see to a job that any of his
people could have done.

She was his Trojan horse…

13

TROY WOKE THE FOLLOWING morning feeling different somehow. Lighter. He almost didn't recognize the emotions, it had been so very long since he'd experienced them. Sensed that everything was going to be all right.

His hard work had finally paid off and his business plans were coming to fruition. First thing Monday morning he had meetings set up with the local union rep, a couple of foremen Palmer had lined up for him to conduct final interviews, and the engineers would begin implementing the blueprints that had existed only on paper until now.

Now, if he could just figure out what had Kendall so worried yesterday, he'd be all set.

He'd tried contacting her, but she wasn't answering her cell, even though a call to Mrs. Foss had confirmed that she was still staying at the B and B. He'd nearly gone over there to toss a few more stones at her window, but Thekla and Frixos had arranged for a celebratory dinner that had gone late into the night.

As he'd passed the evening with Palmer and his wife Penelope, Bryna and Caleb, and Ari with Elena, he kept thinking about how nice it would have been to have Kendall there. She'd gotten on so well with everyone during contract negotiations, he knew she'd fit right in at the Metaxas dinner table, giving as well as she took.

In that regard, it wasn't her that he'd be worried about, but rather himself and whether he'd be able to make it through a meal without wanting to maneuver her into a shadowy corner and ravish her, no matter what course was being served.

With quick efficiency, Troy took his morning shower, dressed and then headed downstairs for his first cup of coffee of the day, and to see how the preparations were going for the open house later that evening.

When he entered the kitchen to find utter chaos, he wondered if he could slip back out again without anyone seeing him.

"Troy!" Bryna exclaimed. "Thank God you're up. You're not going to believe what's going on…"

A half hour later, Troy wanted to put out an all-points bulletin for the truck that had just hit him.

How was it possible for so much to go wrong in such a short period of time?

First, half the lights the Bermans had hung weren't working and no one could seem to scare up either one of the brothers. Second, Miss Thekla had sprained her ankle, necessitating a trip to the clinic in the next county where they'd told her to keep all weight off it for at least forty-eight hours, leaving trays upon trays of food to be cooked in the double ovens the kitchen boasted, not to mention the fresh food that needed to be washed, chopped and assembled. Third, the caterer they'd hired had called to report delays of her own, and no contract was going to change that.

And if that weren't enough, while Bryna was busy outlining what had happened, another problem cropped up: only half their order for alcohol had been delivered.

Troy stood sipping his coffee, sifting through the developments, deciding what needed to be handled first.

"Where's Ari?" he asked no one in particular.

Bryna had put on an apron and was shooing the injured Thekla to a nearby chair when it became obvious she wasn't going to leave the room. Frixos looked harried and wet, as he'd just come in from the rain after pounding stakes and attaching red tape around them on the south lawn for extra parking.

Troy noted that only his father looked completely unperturbed as he chose a Danish from a plate on the counter.

"I don't know," Bryna admitted. "He got a call

earlier and shot out of here without explanation. But Elena should be coming in any minute now. She can help with the cooking and prep work."

He nodded.

"Okay, this is what we're going to do…"

"YOU'RE GOING TO BREAK your neck!" Bryna shouted from the foot of the ladder. "Screw the lights. Half of them work. That's enough."

Troy set his jaw and rebalanced himself, wiping the cold rain from his brow as he followed the section of bulbs that appeared to be disconnected from the rest. There. The string was unplugged.

He grimaced, wondering if it was a great idea to connect them in this weather.

"Bryna, go flick off the power switch to all the lights," he shouted.

"What?"

He repeated his request and then waited. The lights that were working went black. He dried off the prongs with part of his shirt and plugged them in just as the electricity came back on, giving him the jolt of his life as he was releasing the cord.

"I thought I told you to turn them off!" he shouted at his cousin.

"I did!" Bryna was under him again.

"I'm sorry," Frixos said. "I saw that they were off and switched them back on."

Troy carefully descended the ladder. "No worries."

He just hoped he didn't have contact burns from the jolt.

At any rate, things could have been worse. He could have been making the wet connection at the same time the switch was flicked and ended up one very large bulb in the middle of the string.

"There," he said, standing next to Bryna and considering his handiwork.

"There's a burned-out bulb over there."

He stared at her.

"Right. I think I'll be going now to pick up the liquor at O'Brien's Pub that Bobby Schwartz promised."

"You do that."

While he saw to the half-dozen other things he needed to before they opened up the doors in seven short hours…

"Looks like you have more than that baby in the oven," Percy said to Elena as he came into the kitchen, dressed for the party in a natty black smoking jacket.

Troy grimaced at this father, who had been little help all day and then back at Elena, whose face looked waxy and pale. Given the way she was sweating, and the heat of the room with both ovens running, shouldn't she be flushed?

He wiped his hands on the apron he had on as the

two of them, along with Bryna, worked hard to get the first of the evening's finger foods ready.

People were already arriving and Troy sent his father to welcome them.

"Are you all right?" he asked Elena when she not so much rubbed her baby bump as grasped it, as if trying to hold it in.

She nodded and tried for a smile that somehow didn't quite hit the mark. "I'm fine." She waved him away. "You'd better get those out of the oven before they burn."

Bryna beat him to it, exchanging the two trays of Greek cheese pastries inside with two fresh ones.

Caleb arrived and came into the kitchen with his mother, Percy following behind them. "Look who's here," he announced.

Troy frowned at the way his father fawned over Phoebe Payne, taking her coat when one of servers they'd hired for the night offered to see to it. He handed it to the girl who went to hang the expensive jacket in the front closet.

Bryna rounded the counter island and kissed her on either cheek before turning to Caleb and greeting him affectionately. While there was nothing overtly carnal about the mild display, everyone in the room glanced away nonetheless.

"I'm glad you're here," she said, taking off her apron. She put the neck strings over his head and then helped him out of his jacket, which she neatly folded over a nearby chair. "I need you on oven duty while I go make sure the girls have stocked the two bars to specification."

"I can check the bars," he protested.

Bryna laughed. "Sorry. I need to get out of this kitchen before I melt completely."

Then she was gone.

"Has anyone seen Ari yet?" Troy asked again, maneuvering two trays of cooling hors d'oeuvres over Elena's head, looking for a place to put them.

She glanced at him. "I haven't heard from him all day. Which is not like him. I've left three messages on his voice mail." She worried her bottom lip between her teeth. "I hope everything's okay."

Troy's concern for her notched up. "I'm sure he is. Patience says he called her at home for a couple phone numbers earlier this afternoon."

He hadn't taken the message, Percy had. And when he'd tried to contact her to inquire which numbers Ari had been looking for, she'd been out, likely getting her hair done for tonight's event.

"The gift bags!" Elena sputtered.

Troy gently grasped her shoulders to calm her. "Are being filled by two of the girls we hired. Don't worry about it."

Elena's mother had arrived an hour earlier and was stocking the buffet tables in the other room along with Verna, who had closed the diner early.

The caterer had yet to arrive, but that was beyond

his control, so the guests would have to make due until they brought the two honey-baked hams, large slab of roast beef and two turkeys with sides for which they'd been contracted.

They expected to entertain nearly two hundred and fifty people, and had set up a large tent with tower heaters on the back deck. Through the house's sound system, classic holiday music would play until the quartet he'd hired arrived to take over in the front room near the fireplace.

They weren't due for another hour. Why, then, did he hear the piano already?

He glanced to find his father and Phoebe missing and had his answer.

Christ, if Philippidis showed up to find Percy romancing his romantic interest...

Then again, what did it matter? He straightened his shoulders. The contract was signed. The deal done.

"What are you grinning about?" Caleb grumbled, juggling trays around him.

"It's Christmas, man. What isn't there to grin about?"

Movement near the kitchen door. He found himself looking for the one person he'd been hoping to see all day: Kendall.

But it wasn't her. Instead, he found Ari shrugging out of his rain-soaked overcoat. His expression looked as dark as the winter night outside the windows.

"We need to talk," he said to Troy soberly.

"No talking allowed," Elena objected, handing her fiancé a tray. "Work now, talking later. Take those out to my mom in the dining room. She'll know where to put them."

That's odd, Troy thought, watching his brother's serious countenance. He didn't like the look of that.

He motioned for one of the girls. "Here," he said, putting his apron on her. "They'll tell you what needs to be done."

"But...I don't cook."

"I'll make sure you're compensated double for the effort," he said, his mind on finding out what Ari wanted to tell him.

He didn't wait for her response as he rounded the counter, accepting another tray from Elena on his way out. But by the time he got to the dining room, Ari was nowhere to be seen. He handed the tray off to Elena's mother and then turned toward the main room, surprised to find it already full of people.

One moment there were just a couple, the next the place seemed to be bursting at the seams.

He caught one of the girls serving a tray full of beer bottles and wine glasses, instructing her to encourage the guests into the library and dining room. He walked a little farther into the main room, greeting guests as diverse as night and day. There was Mr. Clayborn, whose family was as deeply connected to Earnest as the Metaxases, in a formal tux, while next to him stood Barney, the owner of the only filling station in town, in his barn jacket and red-and-black-checked flannel shirt.

Troy greeted them with equal warmth, enquiring about their families and businesses, his gaze still sweeping the room for his brother. Instead of finding him, he verified his suspicions about his father when he found him at the piano, a smiling Phoebe leaning against the side, a happy audience of one even though several couples were also gathered there, singing along with Percy.

Troy thought about pulling his father away, inventing some bit of business that he needed to see to, but another few guests stepped in front of him to offer their well wishes and compliments and he graciously accepted them.

Then, all at once, the morphing crowd seemed to part and his gaze settled on the door opening to their latest arrival.

Kendall.

Troy's breath snagged in his throat at the sight of her. She had yet to spot him, her blond hair catching the light as she looked around. She wore a fire-engine red knit dress that was perfect for the occasion, with just a hint of impropriety about it in the short hem and the off-the-shoulder top.

Damn, but the woman did something to him. He instantly felt both calm and excitable. Every other thought was chased from his head to be replaced by an almost overwhelming desire to kiss her. To fold her into his arms and slide his hand up to see if the dark hose she wore ended in garters.

Her gaze finally met his.

For a moment, a brief moment, she looked relieved and happy to see him.

Then the same expression she'd worn the day before darkened her pretty face.

Troy didn't care. She was here. And that was all that mattered....

14

IT DIDN'T LOOK LIKE Philippidis was there yet.
Good.

Despite the roaring fireplace to her left, and the
general warmth of the house after having come in
from the rain, Kendall felt cold. Truth be told, she
hadn't been able to warm herself since yesterday,
when she'd done the dirty deed and then run from
the mill like Cinderella from the ball at midnight.

Could it be perhaps because the fairy tale was
now definitely over?

The house was much larger than she might have
expected. Sure, she knew that the Metaxases had
accumulated a lot of wealth through their various
interests in the town in the past, but somehow she
hadn't envisioned Troy living on such a grand scale.
This wasn't a mere house, this was an estate. She
looked around, wondering how many wings the

place boasted, how many bedrooms and connected baths.

Debra Foss had thought it was a good idea to convert her onetime family home into a bed-and-breakfast. This would be an exclusive five-star hotel.

A female server in a black dress and white apron offered her a glass of champagne. She considered refusing. Despite her choice of attire, she wasn't there for fun. She had something important to do.

But just as she'd chosen the dress to fit in, she accepted the drink with the same intentions...then downed half the contents before she could catch herself.

So much for good intentions.

Across the room, her gaze settled on the man she needed to see.

Troy...

Kendall instantly felt warmer.

She realized that the champagne could be as much to credit as the man she was looking at, but she couldn't spare the brain cells needed to explore the question. She hadn't slept a wink. And while her expensive concealer and talent with a foundation powder brush covered up her restless night, inside she was little more than a bag of jangled nerves.

She made her way toward Troy, intent on one thing and one thing only: telling him the truth.

"I'm glad you came," he murmured, taking her elbow and placing a lingering kiss on her cheek.

This time Kendall knew that the shiver that ran the length of her arm and down her spine was one-hundred-percent Troy. Within an instant she had tuned into everything about him. The way he towered over her by a few inches. The heat of his body seeping into hers. The tangy scent of his aftershave as it filled her nose. The need that fairly leapt from his dark eyes like blue flame, catching her on fire.

"Troy, I need to talk to you," she whispered.

His grin told her that he wasn't getting it. "My idea, exactly. Come on."

She wasn't sure where he was leading her, but so long as it was somewhere private, that's all that mattered.

The better part of the day had been spent trying to figure out what she should do. Instead, an hour ago, she'd realized what she couldn't do. She couldn't allow Troy to go forward thinking that he'd triumphed when he'd lost. Go through this party in a celebratory mood, ready to conquer the world and give Earnest new hope, when he'd inevitably find out it was all a lie.

But the idea of revealing the truth during such a festive event made her stomach hurt.

Look at them all, she thought as Troy led the way through the happy crowd that was no doubt celebrating Troy's victory as much as—if not more than—the holiday season.

Finally, they were walking down a darkened hall.

She though he might be taking her to a downstairs bedroom or a study. Instead, he stopped in the middle, and then pressed her against the wood paneling, his mouth claiming hers even as his hand reached under the hem of her skirt.

Kendall gasped. Boy oh boy, had he read her wrong.

The problem was that he was quickly bringing her to his way of thinking…

TROY WANTED TO INHALE her whole. He glided his tongue against hers, tasting the tang of champagne there, his own ragged breathing filling his ears. Hell, she felt good. Too good.

He'd intended to take her to the back study where he could close the door, but he hadn't been able to last that long. Instead, he'd pressed her against the hall wall, turned on by her surprised gasp, his hand finding its way under her dress as if of its own accord.

Damn, but she was hot. He slid his fingers between her toned thighs and used his right leg to edge her knees apart, giving him the access he so hungrily sought. His index finger met with the crotch of her panties, finding her wet, so very wet. He worked his way inside the soft cotton, gliding between her swollen folds even as he deepened their kiss.

"Please…" she said restlessly.

Oh, he intended to please her, in every way there was for a man to please a woman.

He thrust his index and middle fingers deep into her, his thumb seeking and find the pearl in the nest of her curls. Her breathing quickened and she seemed to have a hard time swallowing as she threw her head back against the wall, her lips parted, her lashes fringed against her flushed cheeks. He slid his fingers out and she instantly objected, bearing down against his hand.

She moaned into his mouth when he met her demand to be filled again.

Christ, he was going to take her right there. Forget that a mere twenty feet away dozens of people milled around the big room. He didn't care that any one of them could walk down the hall at any minute looking for the bathroom or coatroom or both. All he could concentrate on was his urgent need to surround himself with everything that was Kendall.

It didn't help that she fumbled with the front of his pants, apparently longing for the same thing.

He thrust his fingers deep into her dripping wetness again…and again…then pressed hard against her clit. She reacted as if it was a button and he'd just opened the floodgates.

Her cry filled his ears. He kissed her to muffle the sound, and then found himself kissing her for the mere pleasure of kissing her.

He'd never needed a woman so much. Wanted her morning, noon and night.

And now that they no longer had business between them, they could get down to the personal.

"Move here," he asked.

Kendall seemed to be having a hard time catching her breath.

He removed his hand from between her legs and held her hips tight instead.

"What?" she whispered.

"Move here. To Earnest." He kissed her, forcing her head back against the wall. "I want to see you. All day. Every day…"

She tried to break off the kiss, but he refused her escape until she was kissing him back as impatiently as he kissed her.

"I want you so much I could burst," he gritted out.

"Troy, I—"

"Come on," he said. "There's a study back this way."

She planted her feet when he tried to pull her down the hall. "Troy, wait a minute." Her throat clicked with a thick swallow. "I need to talk to you… Now…"

"We can talk in the study."

"No, we won't. We'll have sex in the study."

He grinned. "You're right. Let's go."

"But you won't want to have sex with me once you find out…"

He pressed himself against her again. "Darling,

I can't imagine a single thing you could tell me that would make me stop wanting you."

Her eyes shined brightly in the dim light. "Trust me. This will."

He knew an instant of pause. As he stood looking at her, he saw not merely her pained expression now, but her somber look yesterday. Remembered that he hadn't been able to contact her. And that even when she'd shown up tonight, she'd done so to "talk to him."

"Please," she whispered. "You have to let me get this out."

Icy awareness swept over him, dousing his desire. He stepped back from her, his hands still holding hers, but otherwise not touching. "You have my complete attention."

A loud crash sounded from the great room. They both looked in that direction as people hurried across the hall entrance on their way somewhere.

"What the hell…?"

Troy let go of Kendall's hands and strode toward the direction of the sound. Where the guests had been spread out before, now they all stood in a half circle around what he expected was ground zero.

"Percy, no!" a female voice shouted.

Troy pressed his way through the crowd until finally he stood in the inner circle. Kendall joined him.

It took a moment for him to realize what he was

looking at. Piano…his father…Caleb's mother, Phoebe…and Manolis Philippidis.

Troy's grimace turned into a frown. He'd known it was asking for trouble, letting his father even casually romance Phoebe Payne. While it appeared she was done with Philippidis, apparently he saw things in a different light.

And had just smacked the top of the piano down to make his point.

His father stood staring the other man down, Phoebe in between them, a petite figure in pink with her hand against Percy's chest.

"Please, stop," she said to them both. "This is not worth fighting over."

Percy pushed against her hand, looking ready to reset Philippidis's clock with a raised fist.

The ruckus had earned more than the guests' attention. While he didn't look, he knew when Ari, Bryna and Elena joined him and Kendall on the front lines.

Philippidis's grin was a little too wide for his liking. "You're right," he said to Phoebe. "This isn't worth fighting over."

His Greek accent was thicker than usual, belying his true feelings.

"Because there really isn't anything to fight over, is there?"

Troy thought he might have been insulting Phoebe…until he looked at Kendall.

"Isn't that right, Ms. Banks?" Philippidis asked.

Only Kendall wasn't looking at him, she was looking at Troy. "I'm sorry. So sorry," she said almost silently.

"What in the hell is going on here?" Troy demanded.

His father pointed at Philippidis. "This son of bitch barged in here and nearly took my hands off with the piano top."

"Yes, well, if you'd kept your hands out of my cookie jar…" he taunted.

Phoebe puffed out her chest and drew her shoulders. "I am nobody's cookie. And even if I were, I most assuredly am not yours, Manolis."

He looked about ready to slap her.

Troy positioned himself so he didn't have a shot.

"Troy…" Kendall said.

He looked at her stricken face and then back at Philippidis. "What did you mean that there is nothing left to fight over?"

The Greek straightened his jacket by way of the bottom hem, looking far too smug. "Perhaps this is a question you should be asking your Ms. Banks."

"I'm asking you."

"Very well. Then allow me to insist that you refer to my attorney concerning this matter…Ms. Banks," he said again.

Troy's stomach felt coated with mercury, as if he'd

taken on the full brunt of the electricity earlier and was still reeling from the aftereffects.

Ari emerged from the crowd of faces. "That's what I needed to talk to you about, Troy," he said.

Jesus, was he the only one who didn't know what was going on?

"Troy, I..." Kendall began.

He held up his hand to ward them off.

"I'd prefer Philippidis tell me this himself."

The other man looked only too happy to finally indulge him. "Remember what I told you six months ago?" he asked. "In Greece, on my wedding day, when your no-good brother ran off with my bride?"

Ari looked about ready to clock him.

"I told you that I would get you. I would not stop, I would never rest, until I settled this score between us."

The floor tilted under Troy's feet, but he fought to hold on, to understand what Philippidis was saying.

"You didn't read the contract a final time before you signed yesterday, did you, Mr. Metaxas?"

He looked to Kendall and then his brother. Both of them averted their gazes.

"For if you did, you would have seen that I now have controlling interest over Metaxas, Inc." He pointed his finger in Troy's direction. "Whatever is yours, is now mine..."

15

THIS WASN'T POSSIBLE. THERE was no way this was happening….

Troy looked to his brother, who finally met his gaze. Ari nodded almost imperceptibly. And then Kendall confirmed it as he watched a single tear slide down her pale cheek.

Elena gasped and put her hand over her mouth, while behind him, his father rushed Philippidis.

"You son of a bitch!"

Troy held on to the old man, even as he tried to break himself out of an ice-cold daze.

What did Philippidis mean he had complete control over Metaxas, Inc? That wasn't possible. He'd been meticulous. So careful. There was no way there was anything in that contract that he hadn't checked and double-checked a hundred times.

Unless…

Unless Kendall had slipped in an altered version on the day of the signing.

Somewhere a clock ticked, ice melted in a glass, silverware clattered to a plate. But aside from the low rush of hushed voices on the fringes of the crowd, no one said a word.

All day he'd been operating in a euphoric vacuum. Convinced he'd finally won a long, hard victory. That the town of Earnest had, indeed, been saved.

Instead, he'd been duped. Lied to. Cheated.

His father strained against his hold.

"No, Father," he said quietly. "Please, allow me..."

And he hauled off and hit Philippidis directly in his big, fat Greek nose...

THE GROUP GASPED AS ONE, a few cheering as Manolis stumbled backward, only to be stopped from falling by Ari, who stood him neatly onto his feet and then shoved him back toward the middle of the room.

Kendall's heart beat so heavily in her chest it hurt. She wished she could have told Troy before it had come to this. Clued him in. But as she looked at his granite face, she wondered what difference it would have made in the end. He would have looked at her the same, regardless. Would have known she was to blame. Would have hated her.

But if she'd been the one to tell him, she could have also tried to convince him she was sorry.

"If what you say is true," Troy said. "Then the contract is null and void. I signed under false pretenses."

Philippidis ran the back of his wrist across his chin, picking up a drop of blood that had trickled from the side of his mouth. "You initialed every page, my boy. Signed it, indicating you'd read every last word."

"The night before!"

Philippidis's chuckle chilled Kendall to the bone. "Yes, well, go ahead and sue me. It will take years and cost millions."

Ari stepped forward. "What do you mean to do?"

"What?" the Greek asked. "Well, I intend to shut everything down, of course."

"I won't let you," Troy promised.

"Yes, well, too bad you won't have the authority. The law is on my side."

Kendall admired Troy's courage. And knew that he would do exactly as he promised.

But in the next moment, she saw something else. A sliver of defeat. As if he'd been fighting so hard, for so long, that he no longer had anything to give. That this had been it. His last stand. And if he lost this battle…well, then the war was over.

Her heart expanded against her ribs.

And she knew a grief unlike that she'd felt before outside of death. But this was like a death, wasn't it? A death of trust.

"Ari..."

It was Elena's voice, low, tinny. Kendall looked to find her as pale as a misty night, her hands gripping her rounded belly.

"Just a minute," he said to her as he advanced on Philippidis. "All this because you couldn't marry a woman you didn't love?"

"Ari!" Elena's voice was more insistent now, drawing every gaze to her.

She gasped and stared at her feet where a puddle was accumulating.

TROY CLOSED THE BACK DOOR of Kendall's car, the only one not blocked in given her late arrival. Elena lay with her knees tented, her head on Ari's lap in the backseat. He was instructing her to take shallow breaths, probably something he'd picked up in those classes he'd been attending with her lately.

Troy moved to the driver's seat only to find Kendall strapped in.

"Get in," she said, nodding toward the passenger's side.

He knew a moment of pause, but only a moment. It was important that they get Elena to the clinic in the next county as soon as possible. And, whatever issues he might have with the woman behind the wheel, she was proving surprisingly efficient in this emergency.

As they'd helped Elena in, Kendall had asked rapid-fire questions, learning that the mommy-to-be had been experiencing contractions for at least the past six hours, although she hadn't identified them as such because she was only twenty-six weeks into her pregnancy.

Too early.

Even Troy knew that much. She still had over two months to go.

As Troy got into the car and Kendall put it into gear, he remembered earlier when he'd thought Elena had looked too pale. Had noticed the odd way she'd touched her stomach. Yet she'd been so busy with the party preparations that he hadn't stopped to consider what might be happening.

If she lost this baby...

Kendall reached over to touch his arm.

"Don't worry," she said quietly. "My sister gave birth early and everything was fine. They can work miracles nowadays."

"Breathe," Ari was coaching in the backseat. "Hang on..."

A glance in the side mirror found at least three other cars trailing them. Once they were on the road, Kendall stepped on the gas while Troy put in a call to the sheriff to let him know they were coming through town and why. As soon as they hit the outskirts on their way to the highway, Barnaby pulled out in front of them, lights blazing, leading the way.

Troy allowed himself to glance at Kendall. He experienced myriad emotions that he couldn't identify as a group, but could pick out.

Betrayal...

Hurt...

She hadn't had a chance to put on her coat, but she didn't appear chilled. She was white around the mouth, but that could easily be attributed to their current situation rather than having anything to do with him.

"Why?"

The question was out before he realized he was going to ask it.

She looked at him. He watched as her eyes brightened with tears. But while he was the one who had asked, he realized he wasn't ready to hear her side. Not yet.

Possibly not ever.

The prospect pounded the invisible knife in his chest in even further.

"Oh, God!"

Elena, louder than before.

"We're almost there, we're almost there," Ari told her as Kendall honked at the sheriff to go faster....

KENDALL LINGERED OUTSIDE THE waiting room where the Metaxases were gathered. They'd first gone to the clinic, but Elena had needed attention that they couldn't give her, so she'd been rushed to the hospital, where they all now waited for news.

She rubbed her forehead. Troy had driven with his father from the clinic, leaving her alone in her car. Why she'd followed, she had no idea, other than she wanted Elena's baby to be okay.

But being around the people she'd hurt so badly just made her feel worse.

But you did it in order to save your own family...

Funny how the argument didn't seem to hold much water now, as she stood looking at the other family pulling together during a crisis. Of course, none of them seemed aware of her presence, everything else in their lives deemed unimportant until one member was out of danger.

Except for Troy.

It was curious how tuned in to him she was. Oh, she'd always been aware of him sexually. Even during their most intense business negotiations, she'd been acutely conscious of him as a man.

But this…this somehow surpassed all that.

She seemed to sense exactly when he was looking at her—as he was now—an oftentimes hard and un-forgiving, other times confused and pained expression on his handsome face even as he stood talking to his father or cousin.

"Is it true?"

Kendall turned to face Caleb, who juggled coffee cups. She looked down.

"I was in the kitchen when it all went down, but Bryna tried filling me in on the way over." He narrowed his eyes. "I already know that it's something Philippidis would do. But you…did you really doctor the contracts?"

She closed her eyes and slowly nodded.

Silence.

She thought he'd left her but when she cracked her eyelids, he still stood there, looking at her. As if trying to figure something out.

"Here," he said, holding up the cups. "One of these is for you."

The relief Kendall knew was so complete she nearly slumped over with it. Not because he'd given her coffee. But because Caleb Payne was a man who would know firsthand what her situation with Philippidis was like…and hadn't judged her harshly on her actions.

"Thanks," she whispered, accepting a cup.

She watched as he went inside the waiting room and handed the rest of the cups out.

Kendall's gaze met Troy's and her heart leapt. If Caleb could forgive her, was it possible that Troy might also?

He turned away from her, taking that slender glimmer of hope with him.

Whatever else she was, she wasn't a monster.

"Excuse me," a doctor in full scrubs said to her.

"Yes?"

"Are you with the Metaxas family?"

"Yes...I mean, no." She nodded toward the waiting room where Troy was already advancing on them. "They're in there."

"What is it?" Troy asked. "Is she all right? Is the baby..."

"She's fine," the doctor said. "And the baby...well, congratulations. It's a girl."

Behind him, Ari appeared, an ear-to-ear grin on his face that couldn't quite mask his concern.

"She's so tiny...but she's crying her little lungs out. They say that's a good sign..."

The doctor added, "She's in critical condition and will be in NICU for the foreseeable future, if you'd all like to see her..."

Kendall listened as he went on to say that they'd only be able to do so through a window, and not to be worried about the tubes and monitoring devices. And if Elena was up to it, they could also briefly visit her.

The family began down the hall. She stayed behind, wrapping her arms around herself to ward off a chill. She was relieved that both mother and daughter were okay, but reluctantly acknowledged that this was where her participation ended.

She'd already overstayed her welcome.

"Kendall?"

She turned, hoping it was Troy who was seeking her out.

Instead, it was Ari.

"Thanks," he said simply, looking perplexed at the word considering what had transpired earlier in the day.

"You're welcome," she said, feeling curiously choked up. "Congratulations. I'm glad both Elena and your baby girl are going to be okay."

"Amygdalia."

She blinked.

"My mother's name."

She smiled. "It's beautiful."

"No, it's not. But it's tradition. And I figure she should have to suffer with the Greek curse the same as all of us. We'll be calling her Amy."

Kendall gave a bittersweet laugh, watching as he offered her a final wave and then hurried up the hall to rejoin the rest of his family.

In that one moment, she didn't think she'd ever felt so alone.

And it didn't help to know that she had only herself to blame…

16

IT WAS AFTER 2:00 A.M. BY the time Kendall made it back to her room at the bed-and-breakfast. Thankfully, she hadn't woken Mrs. Foss while gaining access, but now that she was in her quiet room, she almost wished she had roused her, if just so the grumpy old woman could drown out the incessant voices in her head.

She should change out of her wet clothes. Finish packing. Take a shower. But she couldn't bring herself to do anything more than collapse to the bed, dropping her purse to fall where it may.

What a difference a day makes…

She groaned and lay back on top of the thick quilt, her feet still planted on the floor to anchor her, her mind refusing her peace. Troy…Philippidis…Elena… Ari sharing the news of the early arrival of his baby daughter…It all seemed part of a crazy dream. So outside that with which she was familiar.

What she had done, the altering of the contract, was so uncharacteristic of her, she was having a difficult time reconciling her actions within herself. But what she was struggling with involved more than that. Far more.

Somehow, somewhere, over the past two weeks, she had fallen in love.

Love.

Such a simple word. Such complicated implications.

Had she known...

She closed her eyes. Had she known...what? Had she known, she would never have done what she had? But that didn't make any sense. Mostly because she should never have done it in the first place.

While her justification now seemed weak, everything had happened so fast she hadn't had a chance to explore all of the ramifications. Plus she was Manolis Philippidis's business attorney. His interest came before all else.

Except in the case of wrongdoing. By engaging in the criminal act, she'd placed her very career in jeopardy.

Which presented her with an interesting conundrum. It was in *her* interest to remain by Philippidis's side. To prop up the duplicity. Doing otherwise would be professional suicide.

To not do so would be the same.

A voice sounded from the hall.

She lifted up onto her elbows, listening. Caleb was staying at the Metaxas house now so she was the only guest at the inn. Who could Mrs. Foss possibly be shouting at? Unless it was a delayed reaction to her late return? Or had the bedsprings creaked when she lay down?

"How were you raised?" Mrs. Foss's voice got louder, sounding as if it were coming from the other side of the door.

Kendall sprung up off the bed. Mrs. Foss's bedroom was downstairs. What would she be doing upstairs?

"Fine. Well, just know this, buster. That tallywhacker of yours had better stay in your pants, because I'm not putting up with any monkey business tonight."

Kendall opened the door, an apology for waking the inn owner on the tip of her tongue…only to find herself standing face-to-face with none other than Troy.

The air rushed out of her body, she was completely vulnerable, unprepared for his appearance.

"What kind of girl accepts visitors this late?" Mrs. Foss demanded. "In my day, if a girl dared see a man this late, her reputation would be ruined for—"

"Thank you, Mrs. Foss. Sorry for the trouble," Kendall said quickly, ushering Troy inside and closing the door.

Silence. And then a loud whoosh as Mrs. Foss exhaled loudly, half growl, half exasperated sigh.

Whatever Troy had to say to her must be important, because she knew what lengths he'd already gone to to avoid the stridently opinionated woman before now.

Kendall cleared her throat. "What she doesn't know is that my reputation is already all shot to hell."

Troy dropped his gaze, his frown seeming bone deep.

"Is everything okay?" she asked.

He looked at her curiously, as if incredulous that she would ask such a question.

"At the, um, hospital, I mean. Elena? Baby Amy?"

He rubbed the back of his neck and walked toward the window. "Yes, yes. Everything's fine there."

She realized how stupid she'd been to ask. In order for him to arrive at her door shortly after she'd gotten back herself, he must have left right after she did.

"Thank you," he said quietly. "You know…for reacting so quickly…for helping out…"

This time it was probably she who looked curious. "You expected I would react differently?"

They stared at each other. And she ultimately figured out that her recent behavior suggested she was a person other than the one she thought of herself as.

The one she wanted him to see in her.

The woman he wanted.

She turned away from him; from his probing gaze, from the pain she glimpsed just below the surface. She stepped out of her shoes one by one, put them on the floor and then picked up her purse.

"How could you do it, Kendall?" he asked quietly.

The question hit her like a gunshot.

She absently wound the strap around the purse, her heart beating thickly in her chest. "You wouldn't understand," she whispered.

"Wouldn't I? Try me."

She blinked up into his face, surprised to find him closer than she'd thought.

She swallowed with difficulty.

He spoke first. "I know that Philippidis put you up to it. At least I hope that's the case. But I don't understand why you would do it."

"I had to," she said simply.

She listened to his even breathing as she waited for his response, each second ticking by with agonizing slowness.

"You see, Troy, our family situations aren't all that dissimilar…"

He blinked once but still said nothing.

"Philippidis has my father up against the wall, his hand around his neck…"

She thought she heard Mrs. Foss downstairs banging pans and generally putting up a fuss, but she couldn't be sure. She could barely hear anything out-side her own heartbeat and Troy's even breathing.

"He threatened to close down your father's firm," he said.

She nodded. "Yes."

He turned from her and paced a few feet away, his hands stuffed deep into his coat pockets.

"There's an important difference between you and me, Kendall."

She stared at his neatly trimmed dark hair, yearn-ing to touch it.

"No matter how desperate my situation, I would never have done what you have."

"That's easy to say, because you aren't wearing my shoes."

"What did your father say?"

"What?"

He swiveled back to face her, searching her face. "He doesn't know, does he?"

"Of course not...the entire point is that he not know."

Troy's frown deepened. "Where we differ is that I would never have sacrificed your family for mine."

Kendall tightly closed her eyes and pressed her fingertips against the lids. This wasn't happening.

She wished more than anything that she could nudge back the hands of time to the night before last when Philippidis had called her with his demand.

Longed to take back what she'd done. Make it right again.

But she couldn't.

She dropped her hands back to her sides and beseeched Troy with her gaze. "I'm so, so sorry…" Emotion choked off her words. She bit down hard on her bottom lip. "I don't know if you'll ever be able to forgive me…"

He stood watching her silently. "I don't know if it's even possible."

Her heart beat faster. "Then why did you come by here? Why didn't you go straight home? Do you want your pound of flesh? If so, go ahead and take it."

The hint of a sardonic smile turned up one side of his mouth. "You sound like you're the victim here."

"No, I sound like I'm an additional victim."

He squinted at her.

"That's right. You're not the only one who got screwed here, Troy. I got screwed, too. Oh, while my father's company is safe for now, who's to say Philippidis won't yank out the rug from underneath him next week? Next month? Next year?"

"Yeah, well, maybe you should have gotten it in writing."

She flinched.

His words were no less than what she deserved. She knew that. Knew that she was on shaky ground trying to convince him they were both victims in

Philippidis's scheme. But she felt compelled to say something, anything, to wipe away the expression on his handsome face.

Was it really only a matter of hours since he'd looked at her with passion? As if he couldn't get enough of her?

The pain and disdain he wore now chilled her to the bone…and filled her chest with a hurt she wouldn't have thought possible.

It was bad enough that she didn't like herself just then. But seeing herself through his eyes stung most of all.

"Okay, then," he said. He moved toward the door, then back again, coming to stand directly in front of her. She could smell his aftershave and the familiar scent made her mouth water. For a moment, she hoped he might kiss her.

Then he turned, opened the door and left. She jumped slightly. Not because he'd slammed the door after himself. But because, somehow, the dull click sounded louder than if he had…

17

THE FOLLOWING MONDAY TROY sat at his desk, oblivious to everything and everyone around him.

Damn it all to hell, he couldn't seem to free himself from the numbness that coated him like thick tar. He'd have a thought of what he might do to salvage the company's plans and then Kendall's face would come into focus and sweep everything from his head.

Patience came in. "Didn't you hear my buzz? I have Sanford on line one, Johnston on line two and a slew of messages for you."

How was it that bad news always traveled faster than good?

He had hoped he wouldn't have to deal with any of this until after the holidays. That everyone involved would at least give him that much consideration. If not him, then Ari, who'd spent the past two nights at the hospital with Elena and the baby.

"Troy?" Patience asked quietly.

He grimaced and waved her away. "I'm not taking any calls."

"What am I supposed to do with them if they insist on talking to you?"

"Shut the damn phone off. Send them all over to voice mail. What do I care?"

The secretary's eyes widened.

A knock on the glass door and Ari came inside.

"Hey," he said, wearing a stupid grin that Troy was beginning to think was mandatory for new fathers.

And reminded him of how little he had to smile about.

"What are you doing here?" he asked. "Shouldn't you be at the hospital?"

"Elena said I was bugging the hell out of her and kicked me out this morning."

"Lucky her."

Patience gasped.

He apologized and waited until after Patience congratulated Ari again on the new addition and the finally left the room, promising to intercept all calls.

Ari flopped onto one of the two metal guest chairs, made a face at the discomfort and then said, "If my ass wasn't hurting already…"

Troy grumbled under his breath. "What's that supposed to mean?"

"Well, it's not every day I get screwed. It smarts."

Troy stared at him.

"I told you he'd do it. Didn't I tell you he'd do it?"

"He didn't do it."

Ari gripped the sides of the chair. "What, you think Kendall did this all by her lonesome?"

He didn't answer.

"And what would her motivation be?"

"What does that matter? She played a part in it. Makes her just as guilty."

"Not from where I'm sitting, it doesn't."

"Yes, well, the view's a little different from there, isn't it?"

Ari chuckled. "You choose now to be unforgiving. Perhaps if you'd been a little more wary when Philippidis contacted us again, neither of us would be staring at the mess we are."

Troy got up and grabbed his suit jacket. "Shut up, Ari."

Not even that was capable of budging the grin from his brother's face. "Where you going?"

"Palmer set up a meeting with the foremen we already hired."

"Want a wingman?"

"No. But you could have Patience reroute the avalanche of calls your way if you want to be helpful."

"No thank you. I'm going to be talking to Caleb

at ten with the legal team trying to see what we can do to wiggle out of this contract."

"Fine."

"Okay."

"All right."

Troy ground his back teeth together as he stalked from his office.

He really didn't want to do this. The last time he'd met with the foreman Palmer had recommended, they'd been agreeing to terms and talking start dates. Now he had to tell them it was done, over. Palmer had offered to pass on the news himself, but Troy had refused, figuring he was the reason for the bad news, he should be the one to deliver it...

KENDALL PULLED THE PILLOW OVER her head, wishing the world would just go away. Or the voices in her head would just shut up.

Somehow, although she couldn't clearly remember how, she'd made it home early Sunday morning and climbed into bed, her entire body aching. And she hadn't gotten out since.

She wasn't ill. At least not with a traditional physical malady. It just felt like she wanted to die.

The memory of how Troy had looked at her caused her to fold up in herself.

All day Sunday, the telephone had rung. Since she knew there was zero chance that she'd be hearing from Troy—now or ever—she'd let it ring. Then her cell phone started vibrating on the bedside table. Until, eventually, it had vibrated over the side and was somewhere on the floor under her bed.

Which was where she felt like crawling.

She groaned and hauled the pillow from her face, staring at the ceiling through strands of her hair. Not even when she was physically ill had she ever taken to bed. Feeling sluggish? Somewhere there was a pill designed to combat it. Feverish? Congested? The same. Nothing, but nothing, was big enough to keep her down.

Except this.

She rolled over, staring at the nicely appointed room she'd decorated herself when she first bought the apartment in downtown Portland. Where before the fine porcelain dogs she'd collected since she was ten might have given her pleasure, now they looked like little more than bits of worthless pottery.

She'd gotten her first "dog" on her birthday when she'd made her usual annual request for a real one even though she'd known they couldn't have a pet because of her mother's extreme allergies. So she'd instead received the delicate porcelain collie. And had received one on her birthday ever since.

Now she wanted to crash them all against her pale rose colored wall.

If she could find the energy for more than what it took to get to the bathroom and back.

Speaking of which…

She stripped back the comforter and padded bare-foot toward the connecting bath. She nearly tripped over a roll of wrapping paper, but instead of propping it back up against the wall, she kicked it. It unrolled in front of her, covering the rug and then the tiled bathroom floor like some sort of white rug to the commode.

Cute.

She snatched the paper up, giving it a good crumple before throwing it into the bathtub.

She didn't want to think about Christmas being only three days away. She didn't want to think about anything but getting back into that bed and pulling her pillow back over her face.

She finished her business and out of habit stood looking at her reflection in the mirror.

Who in the hell was that mad woman?

It seemed oddly apropos that she didn't recognize herself. Why shouldn't that manifest physically? Her blond hair was more than a tangled mess around her head, it was a matted nest, and no matter how much she tried to push it back from her face, it flopped back down, knotted in place. Her skin was washed out, her face blotchy, her flannel pajamas buttoned wrong. Everything was just…off.

The apartment phone rang again. She leaned against the sink and closed her eyes. She really needed to go switch off the ringer and check the answering machine to make sure there were no emergencies.

So why, then, couldn't she bring herself to budge?

The ringing stopped.

Thank God.

She filled the rinse cup with water and sipped, trying to remember the last time she'd eaten…and the phone started ringing again.

With a resigned sigh, she put the cup back in the holder and padded through the bedroom to the living room. The answering machine display showed she had nine messages.

She picked up the handset, stared at the caller ID to find it was her father and hesitated answering.

She could feign an illness. She had compared how she was feeling to one a few minutes ago.

The receiver stopped ringing and the ID window went blank.

Which gave her the perfect opportunity to scroll through the numbers that had come in. Her sister… her father…her mother…

No Troy.

She put the receiver back in its holder. That meant that none of the messages would be from him.

She pressed the Play button and went to put on a much-needed pot of coffee, wishing she had her slippers when her bare feet hit the cold tile of the kitchen.

The first five messages were from her sister. Then

one from her mother, inviting her to Sunday dinner. Then her father. Then they reverted back to her sister. Nothing important, although by the end, there was a decidedly concerned tone to the messages and requests to call back.

Kendall squinted at the clock on the coffeemaker. Just past nine. In the morning? Night? She craned her neck toward the French doors in the dining room, unable to tell if it was light or dark. Of course, with all the rainy weather they'd been having, she wasn't sure she would be able to tell the difference anyway.

Night. It had to be night. Despite the rain, it was too dim even with the curtains shut to be day.

That meant that she'd spent nearly three days in bed.

Maybe she had come down with something...

Yeah, right. A big case of the guilts was all she had.

She reached into the refrigerator and took out a yogurt, leaning against the counter as she ate it while the coffee machine spit next to her.

The telephone began ringing again.

She squinted. No, wait. That wasn't the phone. That was the doorbell.

She put the half-eaten yogurt cup down and went to press the intercom button next to the door.

Her sister.

She buzzed her up and when Celia knocked on her door, she opened it and practically fell into her arms. "Oh, Celia, what have I done?"

18

BY WEDNESDAY, TROY WAS READY to give up. Every time he plugged a hole in the dyke, another one sprouted. And he was running out of fingers fast.

Their attempts to get the contract voided were hitting brick wall after brick wall and it appeared nothing short of a lawsuit would accomplish it. A process that would tie their hands until a ruling was rendered, which could take years.

The meeting with the foremen and local union officials on Monday hadn't gone well. There were threats of lawsuits against *them* for breach of promise. To top it off, tempers had run high, with Palmer nearly taking a right to the jaw when he'd tried to intervene in a shouting match between Ari and one of the foremen.

The fact that the men were all locals didn't help matters. Wherever any of them went, they were treated with disdain and Palmer's house had been pelted with eggs the night before.

Troy had believed he could save the town. Instead, he had doomed it.

He sat in his car inside the Metaxas garage following the end of a grueling day. The string of Christmas lights were half out again, but he couldn't bring himself to care. At least the house would be quiet. Ari and Elena were at the hospital and wouldn't be returning till late. Bryna was staying in Seattle, where Caleb continued to work with a team of attorneys trying to find a loophole, a way they could bypass Philippidis and keep going forward with their plans.

Not that they could, even without the legal problems. The company's resources were tapped out with the advances they'd given the engineers last week in anticipation of the investment capital that was supposed to be coming through this week.

And on top of everything, Troy couldn't seem to stop thinking about Kendall.

At least five times a day he reached for his phone to call her. And that many times he refrained. What could he possibly say to her? A part of him just wanted to hear her voice. A bigger part of him was angrier than hell and wanted to demand she do something, anything to turn back the hands of time.

No. He wouldn't be calling her. Not today. Not tomorrow. Not ever. He couldn't forgive what she'd done. Her actions had impacted his entire family. And that included the town of Earnest.

Troy rubbed his closed eyelids and then climbed from the car, his footsteps echoing through the six-bay garage as he headed toward the door and the corridor beyond.

"Kalispera," Miss Thekla greeted him as he entered the kitchen.

He returned the greeting and asked what was for dinner, not really hearing her response, although he made the requisite sounds of appreciation. Something did smell good, but he had zero appetite.

"Your father's in the library. He says he'd like you to join him there."

He thanked her and left the room to go up to his suite and clean up.

Troy had hoped to have a quiet night to himself. A few hours to try to absorb everything that had happened. And examine all the angles to make sure there wasn't something else he could be doing.

But the truth was, he was drained. Completely, utterly drained. Fresh out of ideas with no clue where to find more.

He trudged up the stairs, down the long hall to his rooms, and shrugged out of his suit jacket, draping it over a wing chair before taking off his tie and rolling up his sleeves. Several splashes of cold water later, he mopped his face with a thick towel and then stood looking into his home office just off his bedroom. Copies of the blueprints for the new factory were spread out on his desk, with notes stuck to the banker's lamp and even to the phone itself. This office was better appointed than the one at work, but the business files exactly mirrored the ones at the mill.

He collapsed onto the burnished leather couch against the far wall, the towel still in his hands, staring at everything and nothing.

How had he let it come to this? Had he allowed himself to be so distracted by a woman that he'd failed?

He wasn't amused by the irony. He was always so careful. Meticulous.

A knock came on the jamb of his open bedroom door. He glanced over to find his father looking around his bedroom.

Troy put the towel down on the low coffee table in front of him. "In here," he called.

Percy spotted him and walked in his direction. He paused much as he had in his bedroom, taking a look around, then came inside and took a seat next to him on the couch.

"Been a while since I've been in here," he said quietly.

Troy nodded. "Miss Thekla said you wanted to speak with me?"

"Yes."

Both of them sat there silently, staring at nothing, staring at everything.

With nothing to compete with it, Troy made out the sound of the antique grandfather clock in the downstairs hall ticking the moments away. He was in no great hurry to hear what his father had to say. And, apparently, his father was in no hurry to say it.

Finally, he spoke. "When did you get to be so unforgiving, Troy?"

He turned his head to look at him. "What?"

Out of all the things he might have expected him to say, that wouldn't have rated a spot on the list.

He'd been prepared to talk about the old mill. The failed plans. Even Ari and Elena's new addition to the family. But never this.

"I'm not sure I understand…"

His father met his gaze. "You know, I was thinking about that girlfriend of yours…"

Troy narrowed his gaze, incapable of helping him out.

"You know, that girl from a few years ago. What was her name?"

"Gail?" he asked incredulously. "What would bring her to mind?"

His father sat back, stretching his arm across the back of the sofa. He wore a simple but stylish pair of slacks and a dress shirt, as elegant as he'd ever been with his trimmed silver hair, olive skin and prominent profile.

"I don't know," Percy admitted. "I guess I was considering where everyone else stands in their personal lives. Ari...Bryna. And Gail came to mind." He rubbed his palm against the leather. "She ended up marrying your best friend from college, right? Ray?"

Troy's jaw locked.

"I always liked Ray. He had a way of telling a story that could hold the entire room transfixed until he finished. You two were as thick as thieves. Wasn't a thing you didn't do together. Used to call you Mutt and Jeff," he said. "And Gail..."

Troy wasn't entirely sure he liked where this was heading.

"Gail was a beauty. Always thought you two made a great couple."

Troy held up his hand. "Are you going somewhere with this?"

A quiet chuckle. "Now, impatient you've always been..."

He stretched his neck and waited for his father to get to the point.

"You know, you never did say why you and Gail broke up."

Troy leaned forward and clasped his hands between his knees. "You just said it yourself. She married my best friend."

He wasn't sure he liked the look in his father's eyes.

"Yes, but there must have been a reason that compelled her into another man's arms..."

Yes, Troy could up with a half dozen explanations and none of them were flattering to the couple at issue.

"Have you ever stopped to think about it? I mean, really considered why she would have left you for someone else?"

"It was hard to think about anything else for a while there."

"Yes, but did you really think about it?"

He recalled the holiday card he'd received from Gail at the office and his reaction to it.

"That's a stupid question."

"Perhaps. But it is a question that deserves an answer."

Troy stared at him.

Percy shrugged. "True, perhaps I'm not the one that deserves to hear it, but you do."

"Gee, thanks, Pop."

"I'm just saying that the day you stop feeling is the day you might as well chuck it all in."

Troy bristled. "When did you stop feeling like a man?"

He knew it was a mistake the instant the words left his mouth. But there was no taking them back.

"Careful, young man. You're not too old to get an

ass kicking. And I'm still young enough to give it to you."

Troy grimaced and looked at his hands clasped between his knees.

Silence fell between them again. An apology was probably in order, but he found it hard in coming. He'd had so much piled on his back these past few days, he didn't think he could take a single word more.

"Your mom and I were going to travel the world…"

His hands froze at his father's words.

"We were going to start in Greece. Kos, where her family is originally from, then Constantinople. Then she wanted to go to China."

Troy looked at him.

His father shook his head. "China. She wanted to go to some small place that's barely on the map that she'd read about in a book."

"The Good Earth."

It had been a long time since Troy had thought about his mother. Longer still since any of them had spoken of her. Her death had been a shock to them all. A simple matter of an aneurysm that had taken her in a blink. One moment she was there, fussing over him and Ari and their father…the next the three of them were standing over her grave trying to make sense of what had happened.

Something had changed in his father then. While

he'd cut back his hours in the year before her death as Troy took more and more control, he'd still been a formidable presence at the company.

But after his wife's death, he'd practically disappeared. He'd become little more than a ghost at the dinner table, haunting the rooms of the estate. Ari had once remarked that they hadn't lost one parent during that fateful event, but both.

"What happened to that pretty girl I saw you with at the Christmas party?"

Troy blinked at him. "What?"

"Kendall…wasn't that her name?"

What did his father know about Kendall? Oh, Christ. He must have seen them slip down the hall together. What else had he seen? And what had Ari been telling him?

Then again, what did even Ari know? He and Kendall had kept their personal liaison personal. No one knew they'd been seeing each other outside work.

Did they?

He washed his face with his hands, remembering his run-ins with Mrs. Foss. Had he really forgotten how small small towns could be? Probably the instant he'd shown up at the bed-and-breakfast, half of Earnest had known he was there.

"You know, Troy, you never were as good as you think when it comes to hiding your emotions."

"Yes, well, perhaps that's something I need to work on, isn't it?"

He pushed from the couch and paced toward the fireplace to his left, stopping to consider the photos on the mantelpiece. There was one of his mother taken months before her death. Another of him and Ari and Bryna on top of a mountain of leaves they'd raked.

He caught himself rubbing an empty spot, then realized that it was where the one with him and Gail and Ray had been.

Why *had* she found her way into Ray's arms?

"To the contrary, Troy," his father said, also rising. "I think you need to acknowledge that you're not a god born of Mount Olympus, infallible and expected to swoop in to solve everyone's problems."

Troy watched him walk toward the door. Just beside it, he turned back to face him.

"Your mother and I did all that talking about that trip. Discussing one day. How one day we would go everywhere, see everything."

He suddenly appeared smaller.

"That one day never came, Troy. I'll never be able to do any of that with her now."

He slid his hand into his pocket.

"I don't want you to wake up one morning with

the same regrets that I have. I guess that's what I'm trying to say. All I'm trying to say."

Finally, he walked from the room, leaving his words behind him...

19

"WHERE WERE YOU LAST NIGHT?" Ari asked, coming to stand next to him in the kitchen as he was pouring coffee.

"Merry Christmas to you, too, little brother."

"Merry Christmas. Where were you?"

Troy put the carafe back on the warmer, and looked out the back window at the clear morning sky and nearby hills wreathed in mist. It had rained so much recently that it made the sight now doubly mesmerizing.

Where was he, indeed?

"Why, did you miss me?" he asked with an arched brow.

Ari flashed one of his million-dollar smiles. "As hard as it is to believe, yes."

He lifted his cup. "Can I have some coffee first?"

He edged around the kitchen island and considered

the array of freshly baked pastries Thekla had set out for breakfast. She and her husband had driven to Tacoma to St. Nicholas Greek Orthodox Church for Christmas liturgy, a good while away. Nearly everything they needed for dinner was prepped and ready for the oven or for serving later in the day. As usual, it looked like enough to feed the entire town.

Troy winced. The last time Earnest had come together to enjoy Thekla's food, things hadn't gone so well. What was he talking about? It was an unqualified disaster.

Ari took the stool next to him. "Elena and I came in at around nine after spending the day with little Amygdalia—by the way, you should come see her. Her cheeks are growing rosier by the day. She's going to be a little heartbreaker, that one. Caleb and Bryna got in about the same time we did and we all had a nice little gathering in front of the fireplace."

"And I was missed."

"Yes, actually, you were."

His brother's words warmed him. "I went to see Gail and Ray."

Ari nearly spewed the bite of pastry he'd just taken across the island. "What?" He quickly swallowed and then coughed. "Pass that one by me again. Because I'm sure I didn't catch it."

Troy gave a small smile. "Yeah. Definitely not something I had on my agenda..." He recalled the conversation he'd had with his father. "I got a card from them at work last week inviting me to stop over."

"I heard about the card. Patience said you threw it away without opening it."

"Did she tell you she took it out and put it back on my desk?"

Ari's smile was his answer.

"Anyway, I thought it was long past time we buried the hatchet."

His brother fell silent, staring out the window as he polished off his pastry. "Hatchet. If you'd have told me you were going over there, I would have been afraid you would have buried it someplace that would have left you in prison."

Troy chuckled. "I would never have done that."

"No. Of course not. Because you're too much in control."

"If I've learned anything from recent events, it's that I'm in control of nothing."

Ari looked at him for a long time. Troy tried to ignore him, showing him his profile. When he did glance at him, he found an odd light in his brother's eyes.

"What?" he asked.

Ari shook his head. "Oh, nothing."

"Don't nothing me. What is it?"

Ari got up to top off his coffee cup and did the same for him. "It's just that…I don't know. Maybe it's the Christmas spirit but…I would have never expected you to let go of that control you seem to think you wield over circumstances—hell, and the world."

He sat back down and offered him a pastry from the plate to his right. Troy shook his head, but then changed his mind and took one.

"So how was it? The visit?"

Troy squinted, looking inward instead of out.

The visit had gone surprisingly well. Better than he would have anticipated. He'd nearly turned around at least half a dozen times on his way to Olympia, where the couple had bought a nice house in a new subdivision. But the urge to go back home had never been stronger than when he'd walked up to their door.

Too late, the door had swung inward and there stood Gail and Ray, looking as stunned as he felt... and like the couple that he and Gail had never been. Not truly.

His welcome had been warm and unconditional and had included a few tears, curiously even on his part. And while they were entertaining a handful of couples, they'd graciously excused themselves from the animated dinner table and joined him in the kitchen where they'd spent the next half hour catching up.

Not once had he felt as if he'd been betrayed. That the family unit they made should have been his. Surprisingly, he'd felt happy for them. And had found it relatively easy to set aside the past and enjoy them as friends.

He couldn't help thinking Kendall was to credit for that.

What was the saying? You couldn't get over the last love until you opened your heart to love again.

Of course, he didn't love Kendall. That was impossible. They hadn't known each other long enough for that. No, he lusted after her…intensely. Yes, that came closer.

Even as the thought formed, he recognized it for the lie that it was.

The problem was that the reason they weren't together had nothing to do with a lack of desire for her. This time the betrayal he'd suffered had cut deeper than even that committed by his onetime best friend and ex-girlfriend. Kendall had shown a true waver in morality and revealed herself as undeserving of his trust.

And without trust…

"Hello? Are you still with me?" Ari asked.

Troy glanced down into his coffee. "The visit went well. I'm thinking about calling them in January and inviting them for dinner."

"Great!"

He stared at his brother.

"I mean, good. It'll be nice for you to focus on something other than business for a change."

Troy nodded in agreement. It would be nice.

"Speaking of which…have you spoken to Kendall?"

The pastry in his mouth turned to sand.

He waved a finger. "Off-limits."

Ari's expression was curious.

"Where's Elena?" He tried to change the subject.

"I'm letting her sleep in. Which, of course, she'll be completely pissed off about when she does wake up. But she needs the rest. Anyway, you're changing the subject."

"I'm not changing it because there never was a subject."

"Blocking it, then."

He made a face as if to ask, "What's the difference?"

"You know, we were all aware you two were meeting up outside of work."

It was Troy's turn to nearly spew coffee. "What?"

"Oh, yeah. It's been all the talk. Where you two have been spotted. The bed-and-breakfast…the motel outside of town…Makeout Cove."

"Christ." Troy used a napkin to wipe his mouth.

"Yeah. We've been taking bets on where you might meet next."

He raised his hand. "Stop."

"Why?"

"Because I said so, that's why."

Ari fell silent. "You know, she might have had a very good reason for doing what she did."

Troy pushed from the stool and carried his coffee cup to the sink. "There's no reason big enough to justify what she did."

"Isn't there?"

He turned to stare at him across the island.

"Hey, don't look at me like I'm the enemy here." Ari's shoulders deflated. "I just don't want you a couple years from now making a Christmas Eve trip to Portland to find she's moved on with someone else."

If Troy had still been sitting next to him, he wasn't sure what he would have done. But clocking him would have rated a high possibility.

"Just sayin'."

"Yeah, well, do me a favor and keep your thoughts to yourself from here on in."

Even as he said the words, it seemed as if a spotlight had just switched on above his brother's head. Ari might be a lot of things, but he had never shied away from what he wanted. Even if he'd fallen for a woman promised to another man, and pursuing her meant destroying an important business deal, by God, he was going to do it.

Now Ari and Elena had their first child and were due to be properly married soon.

Troy had to admit that he'd never seen his brother so happy.

The telephone rang on the wall near the door. Ari hurried to answer. Moments later he hung up the receiver.

"You're not going to believe this," he said. "But a mudslide is heading for downtown Earnest—"

"What?" Troy was already halfway out the kitchen to change. "There can't be a goddamn mudslide on Christmas."

"Correct me if I'm wrong," Ari said as they both took the steps upstairs two at a time. "But forces of nature tend not to consult a calendar..."

CHRISTMAS MORNING DAWNED CLEAR and bright after more rain than Kendall could remember. Which was a good thing, because the damp weather was helping her not at all in her attempt to cheer up.

Her parents' apartment echoed with laughter as little Mason ran around with the ribbons from the gifts they'd all opened, and Matilda seemed equally more enchanted with the wrapping paper than her presents. The entire place smelled like the turkey her mother was baking in the oven.

The day was much like every other holiday they'd shared together over the years...except that Kendall felt different. Whereas before she might have been down on the floor playing with her niece and nephew and acting like a kid herself, or helping her mother with dinner, or even chatting with her sister while her husband surfed satellite channels for sports coverage, she instead stood in front of the large balcony doors that looked out over Portland.

Thankfully her sister didn't dog her with questions or ask if she was okay. After the other day…well, she knew what the deal was. And except for letting her know that she was there if she needed her, she wasn't pushing it.

Kendall rubbed her forehead, recalling the way she'd practically dissolved into a puddle of tears in her sister's shocked arms. Celia had been so beside herself at the sight she'd been convinced someone had died.

Somehow, Kendall had gotten out the story. The truth, the whole truth and nothing but the truth.

And while Celia had tried her best to cover her surprise, she'd been left dumbfounded.

Her always-in-control sister had lost it. Over a man.

Then there was the whole contract angle. On that, Celia had been adamant. No matter the consequences, she advised her to do the proper thing.

Kendall hadn't had to ask her what she believed that was. She knew.

She needed to set the wrong to right. Not because she hoped it might regain her Troy's attention. No. She was afraid that was lost forever. Instead, she needed to clear her own conscience of what she'd done.

She'd requested her sister not tell their father. The

fact was, she was ashamed she'd ever believed he'd accept her behavior. He'd raised them to believe that when the day was at its end, it was only knowing you had done your best that allowed you a good night's sleep. And that your word was your bond. You could have all the material assets in the world, but if you didn't have a good name, you had nothing.

She frowned. She wondered if anyone had ever told Manolis Philippidis that. She doubted it.

Kendall turned from the window and walked into the kitchen where her mother was testing the turkey thermometer.

"Where's Dad?" she asked.

"Where he always is. In his office catching a bit of news before one of us calls him back out."

She smiled. Her dad. The newshound.

After asking if her mother needed help and being told not yet, she rounded the corner and walked up the hall to her father's small home office—it was more of a den now that there were grandchildren around to spend the night. She knocked lightly even though the door was open and peeked her head inside.

"Anything interesting?" she asked.

He appeared not to have heard her, so focused he was on the tiny television screen he had perched on top of a dresser.

"Dad?"

She walked slowly into the room.

"Kendall, you've got to see this," he said. "Mudslides all over."

She stared at the small screen wondering how he could possibly make anything out on it. His reading glasses sat perched on the edge of his nose and he had his balding head tilted back so he could see. She watched as under the Happy Holidays banner, scenes from Washington State swept across the display.

"Where are you going?" her father asked.

"Earnest!"

20

THE ENORMITY OF THE SITUATION was almost too much to take in. Troy stood shoulder to shoulder with Ari, Palmer, Sheriff Barnaby, Caleb and a couple dozen other men and women of the town studying the sight before them.

The steep hill behind the western line of Main Street businesses bore two telltale bare spots high up—two oblong patches of red earth bare of pines and normal foliage. The juxtaposition of the clear sky combined with the possibility of a mudslide seemed almost too bizarre to consider.

One of the businesses at risk was Penelope's, Palmer's wife's, along with seven other storefronts in three buildings with apartments over them. And if the coming slide was as bad as they feared, it was quite possible it could flow across Main Street to claim the other side as well and perhaps even the first block of houses beyond. Most of the buildings were well over a hundred years old and would collapse like matchsticks if hit with a wall of mud.

Troy looked over to find several faces pressed against the glass of the Quality Diner, which had opened for a few hours on Christmas Day for those who didn't have family or anywhere else to go. Including the owner herself, Verna Burns.

"If the wind shifts, this is going to be bad," Palmer said to his right.

"A catastrophe," Caleb said to his left.

Troy agreed. Here he'd been worried about the financial health of the town. Now they faced a physical risk.

"What about the state? The national guard?" he asked Sheriff Barnaby.

The other man pushed his hat back and scratched his head. "There are two other active mudslides right now. They're tied up. Won't be able to send any help until tomorrow at the earliest." His cheeks inflated. "That strange drought this summer and now all that damn rain this season…"

He didn't need to continue. They all knew the story.

"Okay," Ari said, clapping his hands to jar them out of their trancelike watch of the hill. "This is what we need to do…"

Troy was given a second occasion that day to view his brother differently. As he stood in a huddle with the rest of the men, Ari took charge, suggesting they

get out to the mill ASAP and bring in every bulldozer, forklift and crane that they could.

"I have a flatbed trailer for my semi," Jim Johns
said.

"Good, good," Barnaby jumped in. "There are at
least thirty of those concrete barriers in the station
parking lot, left behind a month back when they did
that work on Route 6. Meet us there, Jim."

"And we'll send out a crane to transfer them."
Troy said.

Within minutes they had a plan. The question was
whether or not they'd be able to finish the work in
time to make a difference.

AN HOUR AND A HALF later, they had the concrete
barriers in place behind the buildings, the sound of
the heavy machinery echoing down Main Street.
They knew they were running the risk of the sound
vibrations causing the slide and acted accordingly,
but there was little they could do to completely muffle the loud engines.

Troy took off his hard hat and ran his gloved wrist
across his brow. Despite the cool temperatures, he
had broken a sweat. They all had.

Now only one bulldozer worked, shoring up the
far side with a wall of damp earth. He squinted,
trying to see who was driving. A glint of silver hair
and he looked harder.

It couldn't be…

He advanced on where Ari stood with Palmer going over contingency plans.

"What's Dad doing in that dozer?" he demanded.

Ari blinked at him. "What?"

Troy pointed.

Ari's eyes widened. "I didn't put him in there. I didn't even know he was down here."

"Yes, well, obviously he is."

Barnaby stepped up. "I put him on when I was called away to see to a fender bender out on Route 5."

Troy yanked a radio out of his brother's hand and spoke into it. "Dad. Percy Metaxas!"

No answer.

"He's not going to hear you," Barnaby said. "Sitting in that cab is like sitting on the middle of a truck engine."

Troy slapped the radio against his brother's chest and took off.

And halfway down the street, was stopped dead in his tracks.

Kendall.

He had to blink several times to make sure he wasn't seeing things. Standing outside the diner with a couple of others, she looked especially good in all white. Dressy. Hot.

And she was here.

She met his gaze, her mouth stopping in mid-sentence as she spoke to Verna. Her immediate response was a smile. Then it vanished.

He stepped in her direction. She met him half-way.

"What are you doing here?" he asked, probably sounding a little brusque considering the circumstances.

"I saw the news on TV. They didn't have footage from here, but they named it as one of the areas in danger. I had to come."

WHAT COULD SHE POSSIBLY SAY? Kendall wondered. She'd come because…well, because she'd been compelled to. Because over the course of her stay, Earnest had grown to mean something to her. She knew what parts of the day the sheriff would be sitting at the edge of town waiting for impatient drivers, what time Verna at the diner stocked fresh donuts in the trays and took that day's pie out of the oven, could identify the clunk of the morning paper when it was delivered to the bed and breakfast…

Even Mrs. Foss she'd come to see as a sort of grandmother figure determined to feed her and look after her best interests in her own ill-mannered way.

The small town had touched her in a way that her own hometown of Portland had never achieved.

Then, of course, there was Troy and the entire Metaxas family…

She stood looking at him now, wishing there were some way to wash away the past and begin anew. She had an urge to throw her arms around him so persuasive it nearly overwhelmed her. And there wasn't a night that went by that she didn't wake up aching for him.

But as she watched myriad emotions slide across his handsome face and finally settle on stone hardness, she knew there was nothing she could do. The damage was already done.

A horrible crack vibrated the air. She turned to look toward the hill.

Troy grabbed her shoulders. "Get out. Get out now! All of you!"

TROY'S HEART WAS RACING with fear that he wouldn't be able to reach his father in time.

He ran frantically toward the hill that was collapsing in a different area than they had expected, making straight for the bulldozer still working diligently to shore up the wall they'd painstakingly built.

Dad!

He wildly waved his arms, trying to get the old man's attention. He should never have been there. What fool thing had made him leave the house and come down? What fool thing had Barnaby been thinking when he'd allowed him to get inside that dozer?

Percy spotted him and grinned wide. He gave a wave.

Troy was twenty feet away when a shifting sea of earth landed on the bulldozer, rolling it over onto its side as if it was no more substantial than a Tonka truck. His heart stopped in his chest. He was vaguely aware when the river of mud hit the last building, the cracking of support beams loud in his ears. All he could think about was reaching his father, who he could no longer see.

Please, please, no, he cried inwardly as he climbed over the moving earth even as it threatened to bury him along with the piece of machinery his father sat in.

He became aware of others on either side of him. Ari and Caleb. They all dug furiously, nearly succumbing twice to the onslaught as they cleared out the area where he thought the door would be.

The building a few feet away gave, spilling over like a child's dollhouse onto Main Street. But Troy didn't see it. His hand finally hit something hard.

The truck.

They all picked up speed, not stopping until he could smear his hand over the muddy window, making it worse instead of better.

"Dad!" he shouted, on his knees and cupping his soiled hands to try to see inside.

Ari and Caleb continued digging out.

"If you're in there, roll down the window!"

What had he just said? Of course, he was in there.

But what he couldn't bring himself to say was, "If you're okay."

After the new closeness they'd begun to share, the thought of losing him nearly caused his chest to cave in.

Finally, movement. He heard muffled coughing as the window began edging down a bit, then stopped.

Troy crawled backward to give him room even as ribbons of flowing earth moved around him, finding the opening and running inside.

"Dad! Open the goddamn window!" Ari shouted, kneeling next to Troy and working his fingers over the glass and trying to push it down.

"Get back," Caleb said, lifting what looked like a splintered two-by-four above his head that he must have taken from the collapsed building next to them.

"No, wait!" Ari told him.

The window started moving down again and this time their father's cough was clear, with nothing to muffle it.

"Thank God," Troy said as he and Ari reached in, each grabbing one of his arms and pulling. The mudslide must have broken the back window and the cab was full, making their work harder. But Percy didn't appear to be any the worse for wear.

They hauled him free and he immediately got to his feet, looking like he'd been dunked in chocolate, the whites of his eyes and his teeth almost startlingly bright.

Another crack.

All three men turned to watch the earth shift over the buckled building, making its way toward the other side of Main Street then, just as quickly as it started, the landslide was over.

21

"MERRY CHRISTMAS!"

Percy held his mug of spiked eggnog up high, addressing the hundred or so people that had gathered in the Metaxas house after a grueling day of drama and cleanup. Most still wore their work clothes, getting no further than washing hands and face before coming together at the same place they had all left the other day during the official open house.

Tonight, they truly had something to celebrate.

Troy hung back from the main crowd, happy to be a bystander as he considered how much worse the situation could have been.

As it stood, they'd only lost the one building, a couple of pieces of equipment, and they would be digging out for some time. But Main Street was now clear, and no souls had been lost. And he, for one, was very thankful.

His gaze went to his beaming father, who looked

like he'd come from working in a coal mine. He chuckled quietly to himself, remembering the old man's words to him after the mudslide had stopped.

"I'm taking that damn vacation your mother and I always talked about," he'd said resolutely. "And by God, if Phoebe Payne will come with me, all the better."

It was nice to see that the near-death experience had filled him with a renewed passion for life.

He realized he was scanning the smudged and dirtied faces of the crowd, looking for one in particular. But nowhere did he see the person he'd hoped to see most: Kendall.

He looked down at his own barely touched mug. Everyone was enjoying the food that Thekla had cooked in anticipation of the gathering. Verna had brought food as well, along with the wives of many of the men so that the dinning room resembled a mishmash buffet that everyone picked from at will.

No one cared that they were tracking mud all over. Or that they looked a mess. The only thing that mattered was that they'd made it through the mess. Alive. Together.

Ari stepped up to his side, his arm draped over Elena's shoulder. It was the first Troy had seen of her that day, so he kissed both her cheeks and wished her a Merry Christmas.

He did the same with Bryna, who neared him

with Caleb at her elbow, and Palmer and Penelope when they broke through the crowd. And was that Patience? He chuckled as he greeted his long-suffering secretary.

"We never got to exchange gifts," Ari commented.

Troy eyed the others gathered. "I think we've all just been given the best gift we could have hoped to receive."

The three other men looked at each other. Troy realized something was amiss.

"What?" he asked.

They dropped their gazes and chuckled.

Palmer patted him on the back. "Oh, I think this one rates right up there."

More clandestine glances.

"Is someone going to tell me what's going on?"

"Sure, bro, sure." Ari took his arm from around Elena's shoulders and motioned for others to join them.

One by one, nearly the entire room leaned in closer, putting Troy at the center rather than his father. Out of the corner of his eye, he noticed that the morphing left Percy and Phoebe in the corner alone. And the way Percy was leaning into Phoebe and she was leaning back, he suspected that the two of them would be leaving on that trip very soon.

The foreman they'd been working with who had threatened to bring suit against them stepped forward, holding his own mug of eggnog in his big hands.

"Well, your brother and us have been talking…"

Troy looked at Ari who was openly beaming at him.

"And we all think that we can come together, work out some sort of employee-owned deal to get this project off the ground."

Troy wasn't sure his ears were working correctly.

"Repeat what you just said."

The foreman did, and Ari and then Caleb added details like possible start-up dates, what financing could be obtained, and that everyone, including the engineers, was also on board.

The foreman said, "The town got itself into this mess together. And if today proved anything, we can sure as hell get ourselves out of this mess."

Troy didn't quite know how to respond. He'd resigned himself to the fact that all his efforts had been for naught. That with Philippidis's latest stunt, it was done. Over.

"Philippidis…" he said aloud.

"Can suck my big fat…" Caleb started as everyone stared at him "…restraining order." He grinned. "Hey, you can't be in this business for as long as I have without having made an enemy or two. Thankfully they hate Philippidis even more."

Troy felt almost dizzy.

Ari grasped his shoulder. "Whoa there, cowboy. Don't go blinking out on us yet. There's a lot of work to do."

"But first there's a lot of celebrating," Bryna said, raising her mug of eggnog.

"Hear, hear!"

The room exploded with the sound of clinking cups and laughter.

Even through the joy he experienced, Troy was aware of one thing missing: Kendall.

KENDALL STOOD OUTSIDE the Metaxas place. There were cars parked all over, much as they had been the last time she was there. It was dark and half the house was covered in twinkling white lights. She walked toward the door, blinking when the other half of the lights flickered on and then stayed lit.

Strange...

She wiped her hands on her pants one by one, transferring the items she held as she did so. There was a yap of annoyance and she looked down at her companion.

"Shhh...you're supposed to be a secret."

She stood in front of the door and took a deep breath, raising her hand to knock. But before her knuckles hit the wood, the barrier opened inward.

"Oh!" Her breath came out in a rush, unprepared for the move.

Troy was holding it open for a couple to leave. His

gaze crashed into hers and he nearly collided with the couple.

"Sorry," he said with a chuckle. "Go ahead. Thanks for coming. We'll talk again next week."

Kendall stood aside for them to pass.

"Merry Christmas!" they called as they got into a car and pulled away.

Troy waved.

Kendall felt her face flush as he looked at her. "Um, hi."

"Hi," he said, clearly surprised. "Do you want to come in?"

She looked around him to find the hall filled with people. "Um, no. I just stopped by to give you your Christmas present."

She held out a plain, business-size manila envelope.

He looked wary as he accepted.

"Oh, and this." She handed him the leash and urged the puppy cowering behind her feet forward.

Troy stared at the three-month-old black and white Boston terrier and the terrier stared back.

"His name is Spike and I thought he and you might get along well."

He held the leash out as if more afraid of it biting him than the dog, who even now tilted his head curiously.

"I don't know what to say." Troy appeared completely mystified.

"Can we walk a little bit?" she asked.

"Walk. Um, yes. Sure."

He handed her back the leash, ducked back inside and came out again wearing his coat. She gave him back the dog.

Spike barked once. Troy appeared to momentarily panic and then grinned as he began walking, Kendall falling into step next to him.

"What in the world compelled you to buy me a dog?" he asked.

Kendall longed to tuck her hand in his arm. Instead she stuffed both into her own pockets. "I always wanted one. My mother's deathly allergic, so I could never have one. I thought this was a way around that."

He turned his puzzled look on her.

She smiled and tucked her chin into her coat. It was cold and quiet.

"Troy, look," she began, then ran out of words.

They continued to walk, Spike's little legs working a million miles a minute to keep in front of them while alternately sniffing Troy's shoes and trying to run around them.

Troy stopped and turned toward her. "Actually, Kendall, I have something to say to you."

She waited, searching his face for the answer she might find there.

"I won't pretend to understand the reasons behind what you did…"

She looked down at where Spike sat, got up and sat again, his tiny, pink tongue lolling out of his mouth as he considered the preoccupied humans to whom he was tethered.

"But I do understand that you wouldn't have done it unless you felt you had no other option."

She looked up.

"I guess what I'm trying to say is...I mean, I know you haven't asked for it...but, I forgive you."

Kendall's heart beat an uneven rhythm in her chest. She hadn't dared hope that her coming there would change anything. She'd come because she had to. She couldn't watch from Portland as Earnest suffered through a catastrophic event.

Now Troy was gazing at her like he had before she'd betrayed him. Before she'd learned Philippidis's real motives for sending her here. Despite the cold, she felt warm all over.

"You may want to open your other Christmas gift," she said quietly.

It appeared to take him a moment to realize to what she was referring. Then he pulled out the envelope he had tucked under his arm and considered the clasp that held it closed.

"Here," she said, taking the leash from him.

Spike seemed to think the change in human meant renewed activity and did a little twirl and bark. Then plopped back down in resignation when it became apparent they weren't going anywhere.

Troy pinched open the clasp and slid his hand inside. He pulled out ragged bits of paper and examined them, looking mystified.

"The fraudulent pages of the contract granting Philippidis controlling interest."

"I don't understand…"

"Simple. Philippidis cannot bring suit against you for breach of contract, because he is not in possession of the contract in question. And I'm willing to testify to what he had me do, if this isn't enough to get him off your back."

He stared at her for a long moment. Then he dropped the torn pieces of paper back into the envelope. "You could be disbarred."

Kendall shifted her weight and looked down. "Yes, well, I figure it's no less than I deserve."

He remained silent, his gaze steadfast. Then, slowly, a smile upturned the sides of his incredible mouth.

"Come to work for me. For us."

Of all the words she expected he might say, those didn't even rate a place on the list. "What?"

"You heard me."

He looked toward the house, brightly lit on the outside and in.

"It seems my brother's been busy while I've been distracted. Metaxas, Inc is going to become Earnest, Inc. We're going to become an employee-owned business."

"You're going ahead with the plans?"

"Mmm. You want in on them?"

She laughed, tendrils of hope and desire wending through her bloodstream. "What about your mantra of not mixing business with pleasure?"

Was it her imagination, or had he just moved closer to her?

No, it wasn't her imagination. The mist of his breath mingled with hers. She detected the scent of nutmeg and warm earth and one-hundred-percent Troy Metaxas. And she thought she'd never smelled anything so intoxicating.

"Well, I'd say we've blown that all to hell and back already, haven't we?"

She welcomed his mouth against hers mid-laugh and instantly melted against him, reveling in the rush of emotions, the heat of his nearness, the hope that not all was lost and that, indeed, the future loomed bright and shiny…with lots and lots of mind-blowing sex.

Spike gave a little yelp. They parted to discover Kendall had stepped on his leash. She removed her foot.

"Sorry about that, buddy."

He did his running-around bit and barked again.

Troy's chuckle resonated through the cool air.

"What am I going to do with a dog?" He looked at her again. "What am I going to do with you?"

She smiled suggestively. "Oh, I think I can come up with a few ideas…"

Epilogue

MAIN STREET WAS AWASH with color, with nearly the entire town out for the Memorial Day festivities that were also doubling as the groundbreaking celebration for Earnest, Inc. The factory was converted; not up to the original, grand specs, but more moderate workable ones, designed for expansion at a later date.

Philippidis had tried to throw up an injunction, but due to a combination of the absence of the original contracts, and the hard work of their dedicated legal team—which now included Kendall—he had succeeded in only further frustrating himself.

All remnants of the mudslide had been removed, the hillside planted and shored up with a new retaining wall behind the remaining buildings to protect them from any future onslaughts. There were no plans to replace the destroyed structure. At least not currently. Perhaps once the economy got up and running again.

Hope. It was everywhere you looked. From the colorful banner strung across Main Street to the updated restaurant-front that now read Verna and Elena's Quality Diner and boasted as many ethnic Greek items on the menu as American ones.

Troy's father had gone on that trip with Phoebe Payne. In fact, they'd left two months ago and showed no signs of returning anytime soon. Last they'd heard, they were in the Australian outback somewhere.

Ari and Elena had gotten married as soon as their little Amy had been released from the hospital and could participate in the ceremony, cradled tightly in her father's arms as the two exchanged vows before an intimate gathering of family members.

As for him and Kendall…

Troy's gaze trailed to the woman in question, experiencing the familiar rush of need that suffused him every time he saw her. She'd moved into Mrs. Foss's bed-and-breakfast, more family member now than paying guest, and claimed a room as far away from the homeowner as possible. They'd also invested in a quieter bed.

God, what he wouldn't give to be able to back her into a shadowy alcove and explore the delectable wonders hiding under her summery dress. And he would have done exactly that if he didn't have his hands full looking after his dog, Spike, and the youngsters that had gathered around to pet him while she saw to the cotton candy machine, handing a ball of pink fluff to a freckled five-year-old girl who would probably get half of it stuck in her curly red hair.

His hand automatically went to his front jeans pocket, feeling the outline of the item he had tucked away in there. Just two more short hours and they would all head to the fairgrounds outside of town for the fireworks…where he planned to propose to Kendall.

If someone had told him six months ago that this was where he'd be now, he'd have called them a liar. He'd been so fixated on his goals that he'd been blind to everything else. Until Kendall had yanked open the curtains and let the light shine in. And fate and family had finally made him realize that he wasn't in this alone…and sometimes you had to give up control in order to get everything else.

"Cotton candy, Mr. Metaxas?" Kendall asked, coming to stand before him in that sexy summer dress.

"Don't mind if I do."

He snaked his free arm around her waist and pulled her to him, no longer caring who saw…

* * * * *

*Harlequin Presents® is thrilled
to introduce the first installment of
an epic tale of passion and drama by*
**USA TODAY Bestselling Author
Penny Jordan!**

*When buttoned-up Giselle first meets
the devastatingly handsome Saul Parenti,
the heat between them is explosive....*

"LET ME GET THIS STRAIGHT. Are you actually suggesting
that I would stoop to that kind of game playing?"

Saul came out from behind his desk and walked toward
her. Giselle could smell his hot male scent and it was making
her dizzy, igniting a low, dull, pulsing ache that was taking
over her whole body.

Giselle defended her suspicions. "You don't want me here."

"No," Saul agreed, "I don't."

And then he did what he had sworn he would not do,
cursing himself beneath his breath as he reached for her,
pulling her fiercely into his arms and kissing her with all
the pent-up fury she had aroused in him from the moment
he had first seen her.

Giselle certainly *wanted* to resist him. But the hand she
raised to push him away developed a will of its own and
was sliding along his bare arm beneath the sleeve of his
shirt, and the body that should have been arching away
from him was instead melting into him.

Beneath the pressure of his kiss he could feel and taste
her gasp of undeniable response to him. He wanted to
devour her, take her and drive them both until they were
equally satiated—even whilst the anger within him that
she should make him feel that way roared and burned its

resentment of his need.

She was helpless, Giselle recognized, totally unable to withstand the storm lashing at her, able only to cling to the man who was the cause of it and pray that she would survive.

Somewhere else in the building a door banged. The sound exploded into the sensual tension that had enclosed them, driving them apart. Saul's chest was rising and falling as he fought for control; Giselle's whole body was trembling.

Without a word she turned and ran.

Find out what happens when Saul and Giselle succumb to their irresistible desire in

THE RELUCTANT SURRENDER

Available January 2011 from Harlequin Presents®

HARLEQUIN®

A Romance

FOR EVERY MOOD™

Spotlight on
Classic

Quintessential, modern love stories
that are romance at its finest.

See the next page
to enjoy a sneak peek from
the Harlequin Presents® series.

MARGARET WAY

Wealthy Australian,
Secret Son

Rohan was Charlotte's shining white knight
until he disappeared—before she had
the chance to tell him she was pregnant.

But when Rohan returns years later as
a self-made millionaire, could the blond,
blue-eyed little boy and Charlotte's heart
keep him from leaving again?

Available January 2011

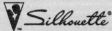

REQUEST YOUR FREE BOOKS!

2 FREE NOVELS PLUS 2 FREE GIFTS!

HARLEQUIN®

Blaze™

Red-hot reads!

YES! Please send me 2 FREE Harlequin® Blaze™ novels and my 2 FREE gifts (gifts are worth about $10). After receiving them, if I don't wish to receive any more books, I can return the shipping statement marked "cancel." If I don't cancel, I will receive 6 brand-new novels every month and be billed just $4.24 per book in the U.S. or $4.71 per book in Canada. That's a saving of at least 15% off the cover price. It's quite a bargain. Shipping and handling is just 50¢ per book.* I understand that accepting the 2 free books and gifts places me under no obligation to buy anything. I can always return a shipment and cancel at any time. Even if I never buy another book, the two free books and gifts are mine to keep forever.

151/351 HDN E5LS

Name _____ (PLEASE PRINT)

Address _____ Apt. #

City _____ State/Prov. _____ Zip/Postal Code

Signature (if under 18, a parent or guardian must sign)

Mail to the Harlequin Reader Service:
IN U.S.A.: P.O. Box 1867, Buffalo, NY 14240-1867
IN CANADA: P.O. Box 609, Fort Erie, Ontario L2A 5X3

Not valid for current subscribers to Harlequin Blaze books.

Want to try two free books from another line?
Call 1-800-873-8635 or visit www.morefreebooks.com.

* Terms and prices subject to change without notice. Prices do not include applicable taxes. N.Y. residents add applicable sales tax. Canadian residents will be charged applicable provincial taxes and GST. Offer not valid in Quebec. This offer is limited to one order per household. All orders subject to approval. Credit or debit balances in a customer's account(s) may be offset by any other outstanding balance owed by or to the customer. Please allow 4 to 6 weeks for delivery. Offer available while quantities last.

Your Privacy: Harlequin Books is committed to protecting your privacy. Our Privacy Policy is available online at www.eHarlequin.com or upon request from the Reader Service. From time to time we make our lists of customers available to reputable third parties who may have a product or service of interest to you. If you would prefer we not share your name and address, please check here. ☐

Help us get it right—We strive for accurate, respectful and relevant communications. To clarify or modify your communication preferences, visit us at www.ReaderService.com/consumerchoice.

HB10R

COMING NEXT MONTH

Available December 28, 2010

HBCNM1210